Life imitates art.

Up until now when I read the Cinderella story, I had always sympathized with her and hated the stepsisters. Now I knew how Cinderella's stepsisters felt. Cinderella could do no wrong. They could do no right. She was beautiful. They were ugly. Everyone loved Cinderella and no one loved them.

Suddenly it hit me. In my own life story, I wasn't Cinderella. I was a stepsister.

I was jealous and angry and felt sorry for myself all at the same time. I hated whiny people who only thought about themselves. So I hated myself for being that way. I tried to talk myself out of my mood. Then I tried to scold myself. Nothing worked.

I couldn't get rid of that mean and awful stepsister feeling. I could feel it growing inside me.

Maybe Madame had been right to cast me as a stepsister. It didn't help any that if I were watching myself, I would have hissed at me too.

— ⬤ —

"This story . . . clearly delineates the sort of struggle that can occur between generations in an immigrant family as well as what it feels like to be an outsider, even in your own home. A strong read."   —*Booklist*

OTHER PUFFIN BOOKS YOU MAY ENJOY

The Amah

LAURENCE YEP

PUFFIN BOOKS

PUFFIN BOOKS
Published by the Penguin Group
Penguin Putnam Books for Young Readers,
345 Hudson Street, New York, New York 10014, U.S.A.
Penguin Books Ltd, 27 Wrights Lane, London W8 5TZ, England
Penguin Books Australia Ltd, Ringwood, Victoria, Australia
Penguin Books Canada Ltd, 10 Alcorn Avenue, Toronto, Ontario, Canada M4V 3B2
Penguin Books (N.Z.) Ltd, 182-190 Wairau Road, Auckland 10, New Zealand

Penguin Books Ltd, Registered Offices: Harmondsworth, Middlesex, England

First published by G. P. Putnam's Sons,
a division of Penguin Putnam Books for Young Readers, 1999
Published by Puffin Books,
a division of Penguin Putnam Books for Young Readers, 2001

1 3 5 7 9 10 8 6 4 2

THE LIBRARY OF CONGRESS HAS CATALOGED THE G. P. PUTNAM'S SONS EDITION AS FOLLOWS:
Yep, Laurence. The amah / Laurence Yep.
p.   cm.
Summary: Twelve-year-old Amy finds her family responsibilities growing and
interfering with her ballet practice when her mother takes a job outside the home.
[1. Family life—Fiction. 2. Ballet dancing—Fiction. 3. Chinese Americans—Fiction.]
I. Title.
PZ7.Y44Am 1999 [Fic]—dc21 98-49046 CIP AC ISBN 0-399-23040-8

This edition ISBN 0-698-11878-2

Printed in the United States of America

To my Auntie Mary,
who took care of half of Chinatown.

CONTENTS

The Amah

ONE

Mary Poppins Time

I never wanted to be Cinderella's stepsister.

Our ballet school was doing the second act for a recital. It was the elegant ball at the prince's castle. However, a large intermediate boy zigged when he should have zagged and banged Mildred into a wall.

If that boy could have remembered the steps, I could have stayed safely in the background with my friend Leah. Instead, I had to take over the role of one those mean old sourfaces who make Cinderella's life miserable.

After ballet class, my other friend Robin was the first to congratulate me. "Now we get to dance together." She was playing the role of the other stepsister, Krivlyaka.

"But I liked being a courtier," I wailed.

"A courtier just holds up the back drop," Leah said. "Now you get to really perform. Madame must think you have talent."

That wasn't much consolation. "But the stepsisters are so mean. Now I have to learn a whole new role. And it's so hard."

That was the worst part. Also, now I'd have to ask my mother to make me a new costume. "I hate change," I said aloud.

I wasn't even sure I could spell the stepsister's name, Zlyuka.

My so-called friend Thomas didn't help things any. "There are some of us who might say it was typecasting, Amy," he joked. I knew it was just the first of many wisecracks from him.

Robin flicked him with her towel. "You're a fine one to talk. They cast you as the stepmother."

I don't think it was possible to hurt Thomas's feelings. He rose on point to make himself taller. "I'll have you know it is a wonderful comic part."

Leah bumped him with her hip. "Just make sure that they're laughing with you and not at you."

Thomas hipped her back. "Not everyone can play a real lady."

"But I've got to wear the bigger wig," Leah said. Her own short curls were held in tight braids.

Robin stuffed her towel into her bag. "Grandmother's taking me to Chinatown. Anyone want to come?" she asked.

"Yeah," Thomas and Leah chimed together.

That only made me feel worse. Those were always

fun trips, and I really liked Robin's grandmother. She was funny and tough. Even though there was something wrong with her feet, she could walk almost as fast as us using two canes.

"Sorry. I got something to do," I said.

"Better than Chinatown?" Leah asked.

"It's just something I've got to do for the family." I shrugged miserably.

Leah, though, didn't know when to back off. If she doesn't become a ballerina, she'll make a fine lawyer— or pit bull. "You're always doing this, Amy. Lighten up. Have some fun for a change. Whatever it is, can't it wait?"

"It's none of your business," I snapped.

Leah stuck out her chin stubbornly. "But—"

Robin came to my rescue. "Some other time."

"Yes, come, Leah," Thomas said, taking her arm. "I told you it was typecasting to pick her as a wicked stepsister."

As soon as I came through the door, Mama called anxiously, "Amy? Is that you? Why are you so late?" She had a slight British accent from her years in Hong Kong.

I glanced at the clock in the hallway. "It's only a few minutes."

Mama hurried out of the kitchen. I was surprised to see her dressed up in her blue brocade with a pattern sewn in darker blue thread; however, her hair was all dusty. "But Auntie Ruby's coming and she expects to meet you."

"You just told me to be back by five," I defended myself. "Who's Auntie Ruby?"

Mama was too distracted to answer. "I've got to have the guest teapot to make a good impression. But it's vanished."

I hadn't realized that this evening was *this important.* Mama only took out the teapot to dust it off and put it back. It was almost three hundred years old and had been passed on from one generation to another despite fire, war and flood.

In the living room, my little brothers and sisters were playing some game that sounded like the Invasion of Normandy.

Mama put a hand on either side of her head. "I can't think."

I bellowed down the hallway. "Be quiet! Watch some television."

Even though Jason was seven, he had never outgrown acting like a two-year-old. "Why?" he demanded, using his favorite word.

Andy, the youngest at six, yelled, "We want to finish our game."

"You're upsetting Mama," I yelled, and was sorry when I saw her wince at my loud voice.

Mimi was nine and a little more reasonable. "Let's watch some Wolf Warriors."

"I know a good one," Didi said. She was eight.

A moment later, I heard the martial theme song from a taped show. Mama slowly dropped her hands and lifted her head. "I never thought I'd be so glad to hear that music."

I fussed with one of Mama's loose strands that curled down her forehead as if she were my giant doll. "Who's Auntie Ruby?" I repeated.

Mama took several deep breaths to calm herself. "Thank you, dear. What would I do without you? Auntie Ruby can get me a full-time job."

Mama had worked nights cleaning offices but she had recently lost that job.

"That's great," I said.

Mama dragged me into the kitchen. "But I won't if we don't make a good impression. She has very high standards. After all, she worked for the Cunards, and they only hire the best."

Talking to Mama was like untangling a messed-up ball of yarn. "Who are the Cunards?"

"The richest family in Hong Kong. Very posh," Mama said. "But I can't find the teapot."

"You moved it to a lower shelf because you were afraid of an earthquake." Kneeling, I opened a cabinet door and took out the pot. Even if it was an antique, it looked ugly to me. It didn't have any glaze that I could see—it was just fired brown clay. There was a dragon curled on the lid, and the pot had a pleasing shape—its round curves seemed to fit my palms nicely.

"Here," I said, but it was so dusty that it made me

sneeze. Apparently, we hadn't used it in a long time.

"Don't drop it." Mama stretched out her hands. I very nearly did just that when she snatched it from me.

Poor Mama was nervous. "Sorry," I said.

Mama cradled the teapot in her palms. "It's filthy."

"I'll wash it," I said, turning on the hot water tap.

Mama held on to the teapot. "Lukewarm water only. We don't want to crack it."

I turned on the cold water tap and thrust my fingers into the silver column to test it. "It's okay," I assured her.

Mama started forward with the teapot but hesitated, glancing down at her best dress. "Not so much water. I don't want it to splash onto my good dress."

Mama did not put on the dress except for special occasions like weddings or anniversaries. I hadn't seen her in it since Dad had died five years ago.

"Let me get you an apron," I suggested.

Mama set the teapot on the counter and then let me help her into the apron. "Some day this teapot will be yours," Mama said, stroking its rounded belly with a finger. "If this were China, of course, I'd give this to Jason's wife. It's a priceless family heirloom. But she'll probably be just like Jason and drink nothing but Coca-Cola."

That's just what I needed: a piece of ugly junk to gather dust on some top shelf. "Since Jason's only seven, we've got enough time to prepare him for the disappointment," I said.

Mama twisted her head around so she could study me as I tied the apron behind her. "You almost sound like you don't care." She sounded hurt.

Mothers. Not only do they want to stick you with their white elephants, but you have to pretend you love it. "I do," I said.

Mama glanced at me dubiously as she picked up the teapot again. "Get the tea," she said. When I started to move toward the tin on the refrigerator, she shook her head. "The good tea."

The good tea was in a cabinet in the corner near the little pantry. "Right." I squatted down and opened the cabinet door. Jars, tins and boxes gave off a collective musky smell that was powerful.

"Got it," I said, putting the tin on top of the counter. "Don't worry, Mama. We'll get through this."

Mama nodded. "Of course we will." But she didn't sound very sure.

When everything was prepared and the teapot had been dried out, Mama made me go get the brats who were all hypnotized by the television. They were all in their Sunday best. This had to be important to get Jason into what he called the "torture suit."

Andy, Mimi and Didi passed inspection, but Jason made her frown. "I told you not to get mussed." She wet her hand under the tap and then shoved a lock of hair from his eyes. "Auntie Ruby will expect to see ladies and gentlemen." Mama made minute adjustments to his and Mimi's clothes.

"She's not even a real aunt," Jason scowled.

As Mama straightened up, she continued to inspect Jason. "She's the friend of a friend, and it's very important we make a good impression."

Mimi plopped down on a kitchen chair. "Why?"

Mama used more tap water in an attempt to flatten Andy's cowlick. "Because then she'll recommend me for a certain job. You don't want the lights to go out again, do you?"

We had lost gas and electricity for an entire week because we couldn't pay our bills.

I put things in terms that they would understand. "No Wolf Warriors if you misbehave, remember?"

Nothing much scared Jason, but that did. "I'll be good."

"What sort of job is it?" I asked.

"I'm going to take another job as an amah," Mama said proudly.

"Not that again," I said. Six months ago, Mama had tried that with disastrous results. She'd gotten fired after only a week.

Mama gathered herself up. "This is different. I won't have six small ones to take care of, just one girl. And these people know what to expect of an amah. They already have a housekeeper who does all the housework, cleaning and cooking. I'll be more like a governess."

I had been wondering what job Mama was angling

for. As Mama had often told us, she had come from a good family and had even gone to college in Hong Kong.

Andy wrestled with the unfamiliar word. "What's a . . . a governess?"

I translated it into Disney for him. "It's like Mary Poppins."

Andy's eyes lit up. "Will you get an umbrella that lets you fly?"

Mama's nostrils flared slightly, a sign that she was irritated. "Mary Poppins was a nanny."

Jason laughed rudely. "You're no Mary Poppins."

Mama defended her record. "After all, I was an amah in Hong Kong. That was before I married your father."

Mimi was jealous right away. "What's the difference? You're going to be baby-sitting someone else's kids," Mimi said.

"Amahs are held in high esteem back in China," Mama insisted. "They're more like second mothers than nannies. In fact, Auntie Ruby came to America because one of the children she brought up wanted her to live with him. She stays in a big mansion in Pacific Heights."

"What about her own children?" Mimi asked.

Mama finished with Didi and took a step back to study her handiwork. "There are all sorts of amahs, but Auntie Ruby came from the highest group. She swore never to marry."

"Like a nun?" I asked.

"That way the family knew she would be devoted to them," Mama said.

Since I sometimes baby-sat for spare money, I was more up to date on certain things. "Do you remember how to change diapers?" I asked.

That had been a major problem on Mama's first day on her last amah job because she didn't know how to put on disposal diapers.

Mama laughed. "The daughter is twelve." That was my age.

"What does she need with a governess?" I asked in surprise.

Mama shrugged. "Her mother died a few years ago. And her father doesn't like her to be alone."

"She sounds like a baby," Mimi said.

"I bet she's a real brat," Jason added.

"Whatever she is, it's a job," Mama said.

Suddenly a new thought occurred to me. "What time are you going to work until?" I asked suspiciously.

"The daughter has tutors, and Mr. Sinclair works out of his home. Auntie Ruby assures me I can be back by the early afternoon," Mama said, trying to calm me. "Now when Auntie Ruby comes, this is what I want you to do," and she began to coach us.

TWO

The Inspection

I think we were all expecting someone who would look like Mary Poppins so it was a surprise to see the plump little woman who looked as old as the teapot. She was dressed in a green polyester suit like any of the grandmothers shopping at the neighborhood vegetable stands. And her shrunken cheeks were rouged with scarlet ovals. She had on enough gold and jade jewelry to decorate an empress.

Mimi and Didi were awed enough by the jewelry to be quiet and Andy huddled against me as if he were scared. I think her make-up frightened him, and it didn't help any when she took a huge chunk of his cheek between her thumb and forefinger and wriggled it back and forth experimentally.

"Ow," Andy said, jumping back behind me.

She rubbed her fingertips together in disgust. "Such chubby cheeks. Too much flab. He should exercise more and eat less."

"Ah, yes, Andy will." Mama tried to save the situation by introducing the rest of us. "And this is Amy," she said, finishing up with me. "She's twelve."

I told myself that if she tried to pinch my cheek, I would slug her back, old lady or not. "How do you do?" I said warily.

She might be as old as the antique teapot, but her eyes looked young and alert. I came in for the most scrutiny for some reason. At first, I thought there might be something wrong with my dress even though it was my Sunday best, but she was examining me physically. "You look healthy enough." She felt my arm as if I were a racehorse.

"Amy dances ballet," Mama explained.

I was relieved to see Auntie Ruby nod her head in approval. "Dance teaches poise and grace. The boy should take it up too."

Andy puffed himself up with indignation. "Me? Dance ballet?" He was about to protest when Mama clapped her hand over his mouth.

Though she was smiling, she spoke through clenched teeth. "We'll discuss this later, dear."

"Indeed," Auntie Ruby murmured thoughtfully. I thought we had gotten a demerit for sure.

As we all went over to the dining table, I said a silent prayer. However, all went well. Jason pulled out the chair just as he had rehearsed and then slid it back under her. Mimi helped me serve the tea and cookies just as we had been taught.

I had expected the tea to go like Mama's other teas where the grown-ups would chat about people I didn't know. I had expected to be able to put my brain into neutral and sit there like a dummy. They did start to talk for a little bit, but I had no sooner sat down to my own tea when Auntie Ruby abruptly twisted around after making a comment on somebody called Connie. Her very next sentence was aimed at me.

"Amy," she shot at me, "what's twelve times thirteen?"

I was good at math. "Two-hundred and fifty-six," I said.

She didn't say good or bad, but without blinking an eye, Auntie turned back to Mama and picked up where she had left off about Connie. A moment later, though, it was Mimi's turn. She stopped in mid-gossip about the new wig of a mutual friend, Sarah, and whirled around. "Mimi, spell 'obnoxious'."

She had caught Mimi in mid-bite, so Mimi almost choked as she tried to chew the mouthful of cookie and swallow.

Auntie had her back to me so I carefully shaped the letter *o* with my lips. Mimi saw me from the corner of her eye and said it out loud. I secretly coached her through the spelling of the word using my lips and fingers.

Immediately Auntie swung back to Mama and continued trashing Sarah's wig. However, a minute later she targeted Jason.

"Jason, which king died in the Civil War?" Auntie demanded.

As Jason picked up the cookie from the plate, he looked at me. All I could do was shake my head. I hadn't heard of any general named King on either the Union or Confederate side.

"I dunno," he shrugged and began eating.

Mama tried to come to his aid. "Auntie means the British Civil War, dear," she said.

Auntie tapped her left temple. "Silly me. Yes, I meant the British Civil War," she prompted.

Jason's favorite baseball player was a first-base slugger named Charley Mason. Since Auntie wasn't watching me, I mimed someone batting and then held up four fingers, which was Charley's number.

"Charley," Jason said quickly.

Auntie tilted her head back a little in surprise. "I didn't realize you were on such familiar terms with King Charles, but I guess that will do." As she started to turn back to Mama, she added, "And don't eat any more cookies, Jason."

She kept shooting questions at the five of us like a machine gun all through tea. It made me think of those kung-fu movies where someone apprentices themselves to a master. Then the master sets them to doing chores, but springs out of ambush and kicks them. The master keeps surprising them until they learn all his tricks. Except the tests weren't physical ones for us.

We must have passed because as the tea ended, she beamed. "Well, except for a plumpness in Andy, I must say your children are positively lovely." She leaned forward confidentially. "Sometimes the children of an amah can be the worst-behaved."

"My husband and I did our best," Mama said humbly.

Auntie shook her head sympathetically. "Yes, I heard about him. Tragic, and you with five children." She glanced at us. "So they were all born in Hong Kong?"

"No, here," Mama said.

Auntie raised her eyebrows in amazement. "American-born children are always such little hooligans." She looked impressed. "You've done very well."

Mama confessed modestly, "It's not always easy to teach the old traditions."

Auntie Ruby gave a sniff. "Parents here usually spoil them and let them run wild. So when Tony Sinclair asked Johnny Cunard for a recommendation and he asked me, I didn't know what to say. And then I remembered the daughter of my old friend." Auntie Ruby waved a hand at Mama.

Johnny, I assumed, was the boy Auntie Ruby had brought up.

Mama folded up her napkin. "Mr. Sinclair? But I had been assuming it would be a Chinese family."

Auntie Ruby laughed. "The Sinclairs were in Hong

Kong from its founding. They were an old family there. In fact, Tony and Johnny went through school together all the way to Oxford."

Mama was beginning to have her doubts. "If you don't mind my asking, why didn't Mr. Sinclair use a regular employment agency?"

Auntie Ruby fetched the last of the cookies from the plate. Mimi, who'd had her eyes on it, looked disappointed. "He has since he arrived here. And the results have always been unsatisfactory. So he decided to get a Chinese amah like he had had as a boy."

"Does he understand that I haven't been an amah in a long time?" Mama asked cautiously. She wasn't going to mention that recent unfortunate episode.

Auntie reassured her. "My dear, you seem to have raised three lovely daughters, and your oldest is the same age as his Stephanie." She saved a disapproving glance for Andy and Jason. "And the two others are . . . adequate . . . with a few minor exceptions."

"Unh . . . yes," Mama said with more hesitation than I liked.

"Once I'm finished describing you and your children, Mr. Sinclair won't have anyone else," Auntie Ruby promised.

I guess we had passed the test after all.

THREE

Little Mother

That Tuesday Mama was nervous before her first day so I didn't mention my costume. "What if the Sinclairs don't like me?" she asked, worried.

I lowered the collar of her coat. "Now you sound like Mimi before her first day of kindergarten."

"Well, I'm not going to throw up like she did," Mama laughed, and then added uncertainly, "at least I hope not."

As Mom started to move off, I caught her sleeve. "Your purse, Mama," I said, handing it to her.

"Yes, thank you," Mama said, distractedly taking it.

"Kleenex?" I asked.

Mama juggled her things around so she could stick her hand into her pocket. "Yes."

"Bus pass?"

She checked the first pocket and began to look a little panicky. "Oh, dear." Her bus pass, however, was in her other pocket. "I don't know if I can do this anymore," she said. "Mopping floors is easier."

Mama was a good mother as long as she didn't get distracted. I kissed her on the cheek. "You'll be fine. Just try to stay clam."

"Now you'll pick up your brothers and sisters after school?" Mama asked.

"Yes, Mama," I said, turning her toward the front door.

She looked over her shoulder as she started to go. "I should be back in time for you to go to ballet class."

"Yes, Mama," I said, pushing her gently along.

Mama halted and kissed me abruptly. "I know I can trust you."

"Thanks. You don't want to be late on your first day," I said, opening the door.

Mama took a deep breath and then squared her shoulders. "All right then," she said, after exhaling. And she sailed out to her great adventure.

By the time I got the kids off to school, I felt like I had sent five children out into the world—my brothers and sisters and Mama. I guess this is how Mama felt all the time. I corrected myself, or rather she *did*. Our roles in the morning were going to be reversed for a while.

However, after first period, I got a note to call Mama at the Sinclairs. I wondered what disaster she'd gotten into now. Had she burned down their house? Fearing the worst, I dialed her on a pay phone.

"You all right, Mama? Is the girl a problem?" I asked, worried.

Mama laughed. "Heavens, no. Miss Stephanie is an angel. But the Sinclairs are having a tea this afternoon and they asked me to stay. I can't very well refuse on my first day. I'm afraid you'll have to miss ballet practice today."

"Madame hates dancers who miss rehearsals," I protested. I could just hear the scolding at the next class.

Mama brought up one of our old arguments. "You spend too much time on ballet anyway. You need to do more of your share of the work. When I was your age, I already had a full-time job."

"You can't do this to me, Mama." I spoke so loudly that the secretaries looked up from their desks.

"But I couldn't turn down the Sinclairs, dear," Mama said.

I held the receiver away from me and counted to ten. We all had to make sacrifices now that Papa was dead.

"It's okay," I said, even though it wasn't. I wasn't going to make Mama feel bad on her first day.

"I knew you'd say that," Mama said, then added, "and make sure you all do your homework first thing."

"Yes, Mama," I sighed, and hung up.

My friends came right over. "What's wrong, Amy?" Robin asked.

When I broke the news to my friends, Thomas shook his head. "When Madame hears, you could be out of the production."

It was bad enough that I didn't get to dance with them today, but now I might lose my part too. However, I had to be as good a trouper as Mama. "It can't be helped." I tried to shrug. "It's family stuff."

Leah planted a fist on each hip. "That's what you always say, Amy."

"Just leave me alone, Leah, okay?"

Leah, though, got right in my face. "It's not okay, Amy. You've got to start thinking about yourself."

Robin knew how I felt. Robin had to give up lessons for a while until her family had brought her grandmother over. I was beginning to understand now what she had gone through. Still, I couldn't complain. It was just for today.

"I'll make it okay with Madame," she said. Madame and her grandmother were best buddies so she had an "in" with Madame.

"But she'll fall behind," Leah complained to Robin.

Robin was good at keeping the peace. "When will you be free, Amy?"

"By dinner time," I said.

"Is it okay if I show her the steps at your place?" she asked Leah. Leah's father had set up a practice room for her at her house.

"Sure," Leah said, and poked Thomas. "You can even bring the thing."

Thomas pretended to wipe a tear away from his eye. "Ah, a family reunion with my daughter. How touching."

"Thanks," I said to Leah. "You too," I said to Robin.

"I've been there," Robin shrugged.

"Ahem," Thomas cleared his throat theatrically.

"You too, 'Mom'," I said. I was glad to have friends.

My good mood didn't last any longer than it took to pick up the kids after school. They started to test me right away.

Mimi jabbed her finger accusingly at her older brother. "Jason stole my lunch so I should get his dessert," Mimi said as we walked home.

"Uh-uh!" Jason said, shaking his head. "You promised me that lunch if I let you read my Wolf Warriors comic book."

Mimi gathered a big lungful of air for her counterargument and started listing debts that went all the way back to Jason's birth.

Then I caught Andy before he could run out into traffic, and I dragged Didi away from the window of the toy store. Both of them sulked and pouted, so for the next half-mile, I tuned out the four of them.

We were no sooner in the door when they snapped on the television.

"No television until you do your homework. We can all do it together," I said, pointing at the dining room table.

"But Mama always lets us watch our cartoons first," Jason whined.

I arched a skeptical eyebrow. "Oh? That's funny. Mama told me explicitly to do our homework first."

Jason squirmed like a worm on a hook. "I wonder what made her change her mind?"

They protested some more, but I was heartless and drove them to the table to work. I found it as hard as they did, though. Of course, Andy didn't have much and started to watch television.

After half an hour, Jason announced he was done, but after I checked his homework, I told him to do it again.

He was outraged at that. "Mama never does that."

I opened his book for him. "Maybe that's why you only got one B on your last report card. How do you expect to become a brain surgeon with Cs?"

Jason scowled as he plopped back down on his chair. "I'm going to be a cartoonist."

"That will come as news to Mama. She expects you to be a doctor." I tapped my pen against the book pages. "In the meantime, get back to work."

"Who made you king?" Jason demanded angrily.

I took out a fresh sheet of paper for him from my binder. "Queen, actually. Now get back to work."

Though he went on grumbling, he finished his work. And he still managed to catch his beloved Wolf Warriors.

By the time I was wading through my English assignment, Didi had finished and whined that she was hungry.

"So am I," Andy called from in front of the television.

I thought of those nature shows with the baby birds stretching open their beaks and squawking—not cute baby birds, but ugly vulture chicks with bald, ugly heads.

"Well, you'll just have to wait until Mama comes back. She didn't have any time to do any shopping," I said. "She'll be back any moment."

"But I'm starving," Andy shouted.

"Oh, don't be such a crybaby," Mimi yelled.

Andy charged in from the living room. "Don't you call me that."

Mimi leaned forward and sneered. "Crybaby, crybaby, crybaby."

"Be quiet," I said, but it was as if they didn't hear me.

Andy balled his fingers into fists and roared at Mimi, "Shut up."

"You shut up," Mimi hollered back.

They screamed at one another and at me, the sound level rising higher and higher. I tried to get them to stop, but I just wound up getting hoarse. Maybe Mama had the wrong jobs picked out for them. Perhaps they should go into opera. They had the lungs for it.

I was grateful when I heard the telephone ring.

"What's wrong with everyone?" Mama asked.

I didn't want to worry her. "They're just playing a game."

"Maybe you should tell them to tone it down a bit," Mama said.

Fat chance. I had shouted myself hoarse to try to get them to shut up, but it hadn't done any good. "How are things going?" I asked. "You're late." I felt like the parent scolding a daughter at that moment.

Mama sounded like an embarrassed kid. "Well, that's what I'm calling about," she said slowly. "Mr. Sinclair is having a dinner party and he wants me to stay for that too."

In the background, I could hear laughter and clinking glasses. It was such a contrast to the battle sounds in our flat.

"But Leah and Robin are waiting to teach me what I missed in practice," I said.

"But it's the first day, dear. I couldn't refuse," Mama said. "You understand, don't you?"

Whenever Mama asked you to do something unpleasant, she always finished that way. If she was an executioner, she'd probably ask the condemned prisoner if he understood just before she hung him.

The sentence always carried overtones of "You're a big girl now." It was tough, though, being a "big girl." I wished I could be a kid again.

But I felt a little guilty. After all, she was being asked

to wait on the Sinclair's guests. It sounded like this job as an amah was turning out as bad as the last one. "Yeah, I guess."

"Order a pizza tonight," Mama suggested. "Treat yourself."

As I hung up, I took some comfort in the fact that the kids couldn't shout with their mouths full.

Getting the menu from the kitchen, I brought it into the living room. "Who wants a pizza?" I asked, holding the menu over my head.

"Me," Andy yelled, sticking up his hand.

I held the menu open. "So what do we want?"

"Pepperoni," Andy said, bouncing around happily.

Mimi made a face. "I don't like pepperoni. It's too hot. I want the sweet-and-sour pineapple."

Jason stuck out his tongue. "That's got too many vegetables."

"Sausage," Didi said.

I tried to head off another battle. "Let's get one with everything. Then you can pick off what you don't like. Maybe even make trades," I suggested. "You set the table while I order."

When the pizza arrived, I followed my usual strategy. I ate a salad while everyone was wolfing down their pizza. That way I could fill my stomach while I was at least smelling the aroma.

When Andy reached for a third piece, I stopped him.

"Save that for Mama," I said.

He scowled. "But I'm hungry."

I thought of reminding him of Auntie Ruby's comments about him losing a few pounds but realized that wouldn't help the situation. "Mama's going to be coming home hungry too. And she'll probably be too tired to cook. You don't want to be so greedy that she doesn't get dinner, do you?"

Andy hesitated and then said, "No."

"So if you're still hungry, have some carrot sticks," I said. "Pretend they're villainous orange robots."

Gathering up a handful, Andy left the table for more cartoons.

The other three started to follow him, but I caught them. "You clean up the table, you three."

"But I helped set it," Mimi protested.

"And if I could trust Andy with a glass, I'd have him do it with the rest of you," I said.

Jason scowled. "You take it easy on him just because he's a baby." He was only one year older than Andy.

Didi stuck out her lower lip stubbornly. "Mama never makes me clean up the table."

Back to Mama again. I threw my fork down on my plate with a loud clatter. "Well I don't like having to baby-sit you all afternoon either, but I had to."

Startled, Didi took a step back. "I want Mama," she said, and began to cry.

"Shut up," Andy shouted from the living room. "I can't hear my Wolf Warriors."

"You shut up," she yelled back.

That started a new round of yelling among the four of them.

After a few minutes, I gave up listening to them and cleaned myself up. By now, I should have been at Leah's.

She picked up on the first ring. "Where are you?" Leah demanded.

"An emergency came up. I've still got family stuff," I said.

"Robin can't wait any longer," Leah said. "We've got our homework to do."

I felt my legs itch, eager to begin moving. "I know. Tell her I'm sorry."

"Madame wasn't happy about your missing a practice," Leah said, worried. "But we convinced her we could help you keep up."

"Tomorrow, for sure," I said.

"That better be true or it's your funeral," Leah replied.

When I hung up, I felt like crying just like Didi.

FOUR

After the Ball

I felt sad and angry all at the same time. No tears, I told myself fiercely. You don't catch Mama crying. She does her job. You do yours.

But if I didn't do something fast, I was going to explode. It was either blubber like Didi or head for the living room.

And that's what I did. The brats were sitting fascinated at the hundredth repetition of their favorite Wolf Warrior episodes. They felt like four albatrosses around my neck.

I wanted to scream at them. *Be good,* I scolded myself. So instead I switched on the radio. As soon as I found the classical station, though, Jason turned the television louder to hide the music. It wouldn't do any good to get into a shouting match with him. With the mood I was in, I could say a lot of things I would regret later.

So I shut them out of my mind and I began to run through my exercises after I had warmed up. I can't say a dining table is an adequate substitute for a barré. However, it was good to be moving my body again. Madame often said that poets write poems and painters paint, but a dancer has to move her body.

After a while, I let the music take over. I forgot I was Amy Chin the stick-in-the-mud. Instead, I was Eveline, the star pupil of the school, with long legs and a willowy body and an elegant neck that was perfect for the swan in *Swan Lake*. She just seemed to float across the stage.

By the time I stopped, I was sweating and aching all over. I can't say that I danced very well, but at least I'd had a good work out.

I had just finished showering when Mama came home. "Where is everybody?" she called from the front door. She sounded awfully happy for someone who had just worked time and a half.

"We're here," Jason shouted, and then he and the others went thundering down the hall.

Mama was busy hugging them when I got to her. There was a shopping bag on either side of her. "How did it go?" I asked.

When Mama straightened, she had the broadest smile I'd ever seen. "Wonderful, wonderful. Mr. Sinclair is so sweet and appreciative, and Stephanie . . . Well, she's a regular little angel."

I started to turn sympathetically toward the kitchen. "You must be tired. I'll heat up your dinner."

Mama patted her stomach. "I couldn't eat another thing."

"They let you have some leftovers?" I asked.

Mama laughed. "No, Miss Stephanie invited me to eat with them."

"I thought you had to help serve at the dinner party, not be a guest." I could feel my indignation rising. I thought of the missing time, the lost dancing. It was like stealing from me. "That's not fair, Mama."

"Did you have a good time at the dinner party?" Didi asked.

"Wonderful." Mama's face shone.

"What did the women wear?" Mimi asked. "I bet it was something pretty. Tell me everything. Please, please, please."

Andy looked at her scornfully. "Who cares? They wore clothes, stupid." The little pig hovered at Mama's elbow. "I want to know what they ate."

"You can see for yourself," Mama said as we followed her into the kitchen. Lifting out a plate covered in aluminum foil, she peeled back the silver sheet. "Let's see. I think this is the pâté."

"Isn't that a fancy word for liverwurst?" I asked, prodding the surface. Make that chewed-up liverwurst.

"It's French," Mama said, "and very expensive. Here's the shrimp canapés."

They were little shrimps on small slices of toast. The Chilean empanadas looked like turnovers. Mama said they were stuffed with olives and beef. Even the stuffed eggs were covered with little black things Mama called capers.

As Mama continued to put containers onto the dining room table, Jason snuck a peek into the other bag. "What have you got in there? A banquet?"

"Miss Stephanie wanted to make sure there would be enough for my family," Mama said, pleased. When she was done, she had covered a third of the table with food. Most of it looked like it came from another planet.

Andy's eyes lit up. "I'm so hungry," he said. "All I got was pizza, and it got here cold."

I frowned at him. "Thanks a lot," I said. It would have been nice to have my sacrifices appreciated.

Andy ignored me as he snatched up a handful. "Mm, these are great," he said, smacking his lips in my direction.

"Don't talk with your mouth full." I sampled one of the snacks. They were good.

As usual, Andy wound up eating more than the rest of us put together. Mama shook her head when she saw me just nibble. "A bird would eat more."

I rolled my eyes. Mothers. "Mama, you wouldn't want my ballet partner to injure his back when he tries to lift me, would you?"

"Well, no," Mama said uncertainly, "but you look like a puff of wind would blow you away."

I patted a hip. "No chance of that." Guiltily, I plucked a spare rib from my plate and put it on Didi's. "My eyes are always bigger than my stomach."

Mama shook her head disapprovingly. "You look like I starve you. In China, fat means prosperity."

"Mama," I said in exasperation and put my plate down.

Mama held up her hands. "Yes, all right. I know things are different here."

When everyone was stuffed, Mama dug around in one of the shopping bags again. "And Miss Stephanie insisted I bring home these goodies to share." She brought out a handful of comics "She's been cleaning out her closets."

"Comics, oh, boy!" Jason wiped his hands on his pants.

"I get first choice," Mimi said, jumping up from her chair.

"No fair," Didi complained.

"They're not Wolf Warriors, I'm afraid," Mama said as the four began to divvy them up.

"Nobody's perfect," I said. I looked in disgust at the stacks of comics. I was sick of Miss Stephanie.

When Mama rose, she apologized, "I'm afraid I have nothing for you though, dear."

Time was what I wanted—all the time the Sinclairs

had stolen. I didn't say that though. Instead, I lied. "It's okay."

While I cleaned up, the brats went into the living room with Mama. Mimi pumped her for more information about the dinner party—what people wore and things like that. Jason was interested in the desserts.

Mama enjoyed reliving the party and told them all the details. Standing in the kitchen, though, with my hands in hot dish water, I felt like Cinderella if she had missed the ball: tired, sweaty, dirty and unwanted. And then she had to listen to her stepmother and stepsisters rave about what about she had missed.

But she did all her drudge jobs anyway, until eventually her fairy godmother found her. I couldn't wait for mine. I hoped it was soon.

FIVE

The Human Eggplant

Because of another party, I missed a second practice, but I finally made it to one on Saturday. It didn't take long for me to feel the missed time in all my muscles. Even though I had tried to exercise at home, it was never as vigorous as when Madame was watching.

Plus, I kept going to the wrong spots during the ball. I was supposed to come in with Robin and imitate the courtiers, but I kept getting banged around by twenty courtiers. I kept thinking that I'd wind up injured like poor Mildred.

Once I nearly tripped Eveline, who was Cinderella.

By the end of the practice, I felt like the worst beginner. And I not only had bruises for my ego, but for my body as well from a couple of collisions.

Worse yet, Madame had said nothing to me about my mistakes. As I once told Robin when Madame was picking on her, Madame only criticizes those she thinks she can make better. Apparently I wasn't in that select group.

I tried to wipe the sweat from my forehead as I limped over to my bag. "I don't think I can lie down for a week. I hurt all over. I feel like a bumper car."

"Don't say I didn't warn you," Leah said. I'm sure she had a cousin on the Titanic after the iceberg hit it who told everyone that she knew a boat this big couldn't float.

"We'll call you the Human Eggplant because you're all purple from your bruises." Thomas grinned.

Robin was more sympathetic. "Try soaking in a tub of hot water."

"Yeah, I—" I began to say when Madame called me over.

My friends fell silent, watching anxiously as I walked slowly toward Madame. It was the moment I had been dreading. "Yes, Madame?"

Madame put her hands behind her back. "Robin tells me you have much to do for your family."

"It's just temporary, Madame," I said hurriedly.

"Family is important, of course, but so is the dance," said Madame. "You cannot fall behind so much."

"Yes, Madame," I said meekly. "I'll really practice now that I know the steps and the blocking."

"I know you will. You are a hard worker, but that is not what worries me the most," Madame said. "You and Robin have roles as difficult as Eveline's. You must be awkward enough to be funny and yet graceful enough to still be dancers."

As far as I could see, I was just someone for the audience to hiss at, but I said respectfully, "Yes, Madame."

"Right now, you are pretending to be the class clown." Madame flailed her arms at the air and then suddenly stood straight and tall and proud. "But you must believe you really are the best and prettiest even when everyone else knows you are not."

I didn't have a clue to what she was saying, but I was afraid to ask for a more detailed explanation. "Yes, Madame."

"Think about what I have told you." Madame nodded her head in dismissal. "I'm depending on you."

"Yes, Madame," I said respectfully.

As we left the school, Leah had to add her two bits. "You've got to stand up to your mom. You can't keep missing ballet."

Robin tried to defend me. She knew how it worked for older sisters in Chinese families. "She can't help it if her mother has an emergency."

Leah, though, only understood the way American families worked. "But you don't want to repeat today," Leah protested. She had a talent for stating the obvious. "You don't want to wind up like Robin that time."

Robin had lost a role as Red Riding Hood because

she had left a practice early without Madame's permission. Ironically, I'd gotten her role.

I was suddenly mad—not at Leah, but at my whole rotten life. "Of course not. But I don't always have a choice."

Robin heard the frustration in my voice. "Cool it, Leah."

Leah still wanted to argue. "But—"

"I said cool it," Robin snapped.

Thomas put his hands on Leah's shoulders and began to massage her shoulders. "Take it easy, killer. You'll get her in the next round."

"I didn't mean to fight with you," Leah said. That was as much of an apology as I would get from her. "It's just that we all miss you at practice."

"And I miss being there." I tried to control the sadness. Sorrow could lead to resentment and resentment to anger. And I had to be good. Cinderella didn't run away. She stayed and did her job.

Thomas threw an arm around my shoulders. "I missed you especially," he said, and then jerked a thumb first at Leah, and then Robin. "These two are no fun to tease. They don't get indignant enough."

Despite everything, I had to smile at that. "Wasn't Eveline great?"

Leah's voice changed as she remembered. Eveline's dancing had that effect on all of us. "She's so wonderful. She always makes me feel so clumsy and ordinary."

I nodded in agreement. "Do you know when she's going to try out for the San Francisco Ballet School?"

"She says she's not ready to leave Madame yet," Robin shrugged.

Madame could drive you to the point of tears when she demanded yet another practice when your legs were already rubbery as noodles. However, there were many times when I felt like a baby chick tucked under the wing of her mother. "Yeah, I know how she feels," I said. "Ballet is like our second family."

Leah laughed. "With Madame as Big Mama."

"Speaking of Big Mama, I've got to go," I said. On the way home, I thought about how I couldn't lose my ballet family.

On Sunday evening, Mama came into my room. "That was Mr. Sinclair on the telephone. He asked me to keep Miss Stephanie company a little longer tomorrow. You'll have to miss another ballet class."

"Will you be home late like last week?" I asked suspiciously.

"I don't know. Don't make any plans," Mama said, and chucked me under the chin. "Oh, now, don't put on that pouty face. You should be glad I'm getting on so well with the Sinclairs."

I thought about what Leah had said about standing up to Mama. "Mama, you said the long hours were only temporary," I reminded her.

Mama wasn't used to explaining her orders. "I'm sorry, dear, but this is how I pay for your lessons."

"It doesn't do any good if I can't go to them," I said. "Ballet's really important to me."

"Going to school, eating—those are the important things," Mama insisted. "When I was your age—"

I can't tell you how many times I had heard the story. "You had to drop out of school to work," I said wearily. "Even then you could only eat one meal a day."

"I'm asking a lot less of you than my parents asked of me," Mama sighed.

Unimpressed, I folded my arms across my stomach. "That was in China. We're in America now. None of my friends have to give up their lives."

Mama grinned as if she thought she had me. "Miss Stephanie's an American, but she doesn't complain when her father asks her to do something."

Neither would I if we had the Sinclair's money. Then Mama wouldn't have to work—and I could have a life. "Miss Stephanie doesn't have to give up everything to watch her brothers and sisters."

"Miss Stephanie would be just as sweet even if she was poor," Mama said.

"Then get her to baby-sit," I snapped.

Mama stared at me sadly, massaging her forehead as if she had a headache. "Sometimes I just don't understand you."

Suddenly I felt bad. As much as I wanted to keep my

role, a stubborn daughter was the last thing Mama needed.

"I'm sorry, Mama," I said. "I'll do it."

Mama nodded her head. "That's more like it." No thank you's. Not even a pat on the head, but that was Mama.

The next day at school, when I broke the news to my friends, Leah got on my case like I knew she would. "But you told us that you wouldn't miss any more."

"This'll be the last time," I said. I hoped that was true.

Leah looked like she was going to argue, but Robin held up a hand. "We'll try to make Madame understand."

"Thanks," I said.

If the kids were bad last time, they were horrors this time. No matter how much I argued, I couldn't get Jason to do his homework.

"No," he said as he sat stubbornly in front of the television.

Short of hitting him, there was only one other threat. "I'll tell Mama when she gets home."

"Go ahead," Jason said. "I'll tell her how you shouted at us."

That rocked me back on my heels. "I didn't shout at you."

Mimi and Didi were at the dining table doing their homework. "Yes, you did."

I sulked back to the table. "All right," I said to Jason. "Grow up stupid."

"You're the stupid one," Jason said, his eyes fastened on the Wolf Warriors. "All you care about is that stupid ballet."

I almost gave him something to really complain about by throwing a book at him, but I managed to control myself. However, I broke three pencils because I wrote so hard in my workbooks.

The fun really began when Mimi and Didi finished their homework and they could devote their full time to fighting with Jason and Andy. The argument started over some trivial thing like which recorded episode of the Wolf Warriors to watch. It only took them five minutes to reach the sound level of a jet plane ready for take off.

I tried to shut them out like I had the last time, but I felt like I was trying to read while sitting in the middle of a circus. After I had struggled through the last page of the assignment, I got up to do my exercises.

This time they didn't even wait for me to turn on the radio before they increased the volume on the television. I tried to ignore that too as I did the exercises. If I didn't do them, I knew I would feel it the next time I tried to dance for ballet.

However, all the fighting had just been a preliminary bout to dinner.

Andy folded his arms stubbornly. "I don't want pizza. I want Mama to bring home food."

"I don't know what time Mama will be home," I said in exasperation. "So it's pizza or nothing."

"Then it's nothing," Andy pouted.

Mimi was more practical. "Then let's order an all-mushroom pizza."

That got Andy out of his sulk. "I hate mushrooms."

"But you aren't going to eat it," Mimi said matter-of-factly.

"Don't be a pig," Andy said angrily.

"It takes one to know one." Mimi mashed her nose up with a thumb. "Oink, oink."

That set them off again, so I ordered a pizza with everything like I did last time with a salad for me.

That made me a target when the pizza arrived because this time none of them liked it. I just sat there, trying to tell myself I was a stone on a beach and all the complaints and insults were just like harmless surf bouncing off my sides.

I noticed, however, that Andy ate his share between insults. So did the other three brats.

SIX

The Oldest Child

They were just finishing up when the door bell rang. "Oh, boy! That's Mama. I'm still hungry," Andy said, bouncing off his chair.

"Mama has keys," I said. "Why would she ring her own bell?"

Andy looked at me over his shoulder as he galloped away. "Maybe she's got so many bags of food she can't get to her purse."

"I get first choice," Mimi said, running after him.

"That's not fair," Didi shouted, following them.

"No, I said first choice," Jason said. "You just didn't hear me."

The four of them quarreled all the way to the door.

"Is Amy home?" I heard Robin ask.

The kids came slouching back. "It's your stupid friends," Andy said, and they went back to watching cartoons.

Robin was still in her practice clothes, though Leah had pulled sweats over her legs. "What are you guys doing here?"

"Madame wasn't too happy that you missed practice again," Robin said.

Leah sat down in a dining room chair. "She appointed Kim as the understudy to Cynthia."

I scratched my head. "But Cynthia's my understudy. That's two understudies."

"Not if you get replaced," Leah said. "That's why we came by. We think one more missed practice and you're history."

Robin tried to find the silver lining. "Cynthia's not half as good as you."

Leah giggled. "She stepped on Thomas's toes three times and kicked Prince Charming in the mouth once when he was trying to put the slipper on her foot."

I was just starting to clear away the pizza from the dining room when I heard Mama at the front door. "What'd you bring us, Mama?" Jason called as he ran to greet her.

"How come you're not in your pajamas?" I heard her ask.

When I rolled my eyes, Robin took my hand and gave it a sympathetic squeeze.

Mama waddled into the dining room with a shopping bag in either hand. "Hello, Robin and Leah. What are you doing here?"

"We came by to see how Amy was doing, Mrs. Chin," Robin said.

"I thought you had to stay for another dinner," I said resentfully.

"Mr. Sinclair's guests canceled in the last moment. So I just had an early tea with Miss Stephanie. I'm sorry, dear. No goodies tonight."

"Aw," Andy said sadly.

Mama patted him on the head. "But Miss Stephanie wouldn't let me go home empty-handed."

"More comic books," Didi said, and raced the other three to be the first to the shopping bag.

"It's just clothes," Jason complained, peeking into the bag.

"Miss Stephanie felt bad that you didn't get something, Amy," Mama explained. "So she did some early spring cleaning in her closet." Mama took out a white, short-sleeved blouse with lace around the collar. "This is almost like new. I doubt if she wore it more than a few times."

Leah leaned over and fingered the label inside the collar. "Laura Ashley."

Mama made me stand up so she could hold the blouse against me. "You're a little shorter than she is, but I can take it in."

"I don't want her hand-me-downs," I said sullenly.

Mama compared my waist to the blouse's. "You don't want to hurt Miss Stephanie's feelings."

"If you don't want it, I'll take it," Leah said.

I would have given it to her if it hadn't been for Mama. I made a note to make it a permanent loan later.

There were more designer labels in the bag. "What great perks," Robin sighed as she held a skirt against her waist. "The only freebies my mother gets are adding machine tapes."

"How is she anyway? I never see her anymore," Mama said, rummaging around in the bag.

"She's been pretty busy," Robin said. She tried to stand so she could see her reflection in the window.

"She makes me look so lazy in comparison," Mama said. She went over to the corner where her sewing machine sat.

Leah was looking at a pair of slacks. "You'd never catch me giving away these clothes."

"Miss Stephanie has a big heart," Mama said proudly. I'd never heard that pride when she talked about me.

I felt hurt. "She must have a closet the size of Las Vegas," I said.

Mama turned with a puzzled frown. "What's gotten into you?"

From the corner of my eye, I saw Leah give me an encouraging nod. "I told you. I miss my classes."

Mama sighed. "Well, I think you should write a thank-you note."

I dug in my heels. "I've got stuff to do. Maybe later."

"Now," Mama insisted.

Robin draped the skirt over a chair. "I think we'd better go."

"But . . ." Leah began and then saw my face. "I've got to go too," she said, putting down the slacks.

"See you tomorrow?" I asked, feeling bad.

"Sure," Leah said. "But Madame will want you in class tomorrow."

I turned to Mama. She was now sitting at the sewing machine. "I can't make any promises. The Sinclairs have to keep their good impression of me. Otherwise no more banquets and free clothes, no more comic books, no more salary." She paused for effect. "And no more ballet lessons."

"Find another baby sitter?" I begged.

Jason saw his opportunity. "I want a baby sitter. Amy shouts at me."

"Fine," I snapped. "Maybe she can get you to do your homework." I turned to Mama. "That's why I was shouting at him."

It was embarrassing to have this all come out in front of my friends.

Instead of blaming Jason, though, Mama blamed me. "You were supposed to get him to do his homework."

"He won't listen to me," I said.

"Not if you shout at him," Mama said.

That was when Robin rode to the rescue. "Maybe I

could ask my Grandmother to baby-sit on the days we have practice."

I thought of the swarm of locusts that were my brothers and sisters. "There are an awful lot of them."

"My grandmother loves kids," Robin shrugged. "The more the merrier."

"Mama?" I asked hopefully.

Mama started threading her machine. "Your grandmother wouldn't mind?"

Robin laughed. "No, she likes the Wolf Warriors. She's got to watch my brother Ian anyway."

"Thanks, you're a lifesaver," I said, giving her a fervent hug.

"I know what it's like to miss Madame," Robin said.

As soon as I had escorted them to the door, Mama called me back to the dining room. "What's wrong with you?" she demanded.

"Nothing," I said.

Mama's foot hit the pedal, and the sewing machine hummed. "There must be something wrong. Is it the clothes? Your friends liked them."

I could feel this ache inside. I wanted to tell Mama about the feeling. I wanted her to make it go away.

"This Stephanie . . . ," I struggled to find the words. "Well, all you do is rave about her."

Mama went on sewing. Her logic was as mechanical as the machine's needle. "Miss Stephanie is special. You come back raving about Madame all the time, but you don't find me making snide comments about her."

I tried to edge closer to Mama, wanting her warmth. "But this is different, Mama."

Mama clicked her tongue in exasperation and then her elbow swung up and shoved me away with a sharp poke. "Stand back. You made me do this seam crooked."

As pokes went, it wasn't much. I'd had harder ones on the bus or in the cafeteria line. And yet I felt the spot burning on my side as I stepped back. "I bet you don't tell that to Stephanie."

Mama emphasized the first word as she got out her scissors from a drawer beneath the sewing machine. "*Miss* Stephanie does what I tell her."

I thought of the long hours baby-sitting and the sacrifices about my dancing. "I do what you tell me to do."

"I don't understand American children. If I'd refused to do what I was told when I was your age, my mother would have boxed off my ears." She cut the thread along the seam.

It's one thing to make sacrifices, but it's another to have no one appreciate them. Finally, I had a name for the ache inside. "Mama, don't you love me?"

Mama's head reared up in shock. I felt like a wizard who had conjured up a powerful, willful dragon and was beginning to regret it. Biting back her words, Mama's head bent suddenly. With her long fingernails, she began to pluck the thread out. When she spoke, it was in a shaky voice. "Don't I work day and night to feed you, to clothe you, to send you to that expensive ballet school?"

"Yes," I mumbled.

"I don't know how you can ask that question then," Mama said.

"You still didn't answer me," I said sullenly.

Mama shut her eyes so quickly that I thought she had cut herself somehow, but she was praying for strength, I guess. "I want you to write a thank-you note."

I thought I had my answer. If Miss Stephanie had asked her, Mama would have told her she loved her.

"You didn't tell my brothers and sisters to write notes," I said angrily.

"That was just for comic books. These are expensive clothes," Mama said.

So I got a sheet of paper and wrote down, "Thanks."

Mama looked annoyed. "Write down what I say."

I wanted to ask her why she didn't just write the note herself, but I knew I was on thin ice already. So I got out a second sheet of paper.

"Thank you for all the clothes," Mama dictated. "It was so kind—"

"Wait a moment," I said, trying to keep up.

The note went on for a paragraph and had me doing everything but offer to kiss Miss Stephanie's shoe in gratitude.

"Sign it," Mama said finally.

I scrawled my name and then threw the pen down. I was really sick of Stephanie now.

"May I leave now?" I asked.

Mama gave a curt nod as she folded up the note carefully.

I slunk into my room. As soon as I had shut the door, I got ready to give off an angry scream. However, I caught myself in time. All I needed was for the neighbors to complain. Punching my pillow only helped a little bit.

So I held it in. *Be good,* I told myself. *Behave.*

It seemed like I had been telling myself that all my life. I couldn't remember ever throwing a tantrum like other children. I couldn't recall even getting to be a child when I was with Mama. She expected me to be an adult as soon as I could walk.

It made me feel . . . well, old. And tired. And sick.

I felt like I was trapped in a cage.

SEVEN

The Living Doll

Over the next few weeks, Mama kept stuffing Stephanie down my throat—literally. One night it was huge hero sandwiches. Another night it was Moroccan food. Andy was in hog heaven.

Some nights it wasn't food, but toys and games that seemed brand new—like she hadn't played with them at all. I wondered just how rich she was. One night it was even bright purple balloons for Didi.

"My favorite color," Didi said as she began to blow them up.

Mama nodded. "Miss Stephanie asked me." She looked as pleased as if the balloons were made out of gold. Not only had Miss Stephanie taken away my mother, but she seemed to be taking my family too. How could I compete with her?

And almost every night there were a few comic books—enough reading material accumulated that Jason might not watch television for a whole evening.

"What's this word?" Jason asked, showing me a word that Superman had used to Wonder Woman.

"Abandoned," I said. That was how I felt.

Jason shook his head in admiration. "And she reads these regular. She must be real smart."

"Yeah, all the geniuses read them," I said sarcastically.

"They must. That's why they have all these science experiments in back." He showed me an ad for X-ray glasses and sea monkeys.

"Let me see that," I said.

"Hey," he protested.

I checked the date inside. It was brand new. "Is this the latest issue?"

"Yeah. It just got on the newsstands," Jason said.

"It's funny that she likes most of the same comics you do," I said.

"I told you she was smart," Jason said.

Mimi held up a stuffed animal, a pink cow. "I'm so glad she likes stuffed toys too."

"Yeah, funny," I said.

And I looked at the blouse she had sent me. Someone had snipped off the tag, but there was still part of the little plastic piece attached to the cloth that held the price tag.

And the truth finally dawned on me. "Miss Stephanie's trying to buy us."

"Don't be stupid," Jason snorted. "We learned about that in school. You can't own slaves anymore."

"She can't pay cash out right," I argued. "She's got to be more indirect."

"All she's done is be nice to us," Mimi said. "What's your problem?"

"You should be glad she's so generous," Mama scolded me. "Now try on the blouse."

Well, Mama and the brats might be up for sale, but not me. "No thanks."

"I think this will look very nice on you." Mama held up Miss Stephanie's most recent present. "Though I might have to take it in a little."

I tried to fend it off. "I don't feel like it."

She drew her eyebrows together. "You've got a whole new wardrobe now. Why don't you ever wear any of it?"

"I just don't feel like it," I said, planning to hide the newest addition in the closet. However, I now had so many items from Stephanie that I couldn't avoid her clothing anymore. I was starting to think of my closet as her spare storage unit.

"I think it's very kind of Miss Stephanie to give up something that she's hardly worn," Mama said.

I couldn't hold my tongue anymore as my family grew more and more under her spell. "If I had her father's big bucks, I could afford to be kind too."

"I've met plenty of rich people who never share their good fortune." Mama held out the blouse. "Now try this on."

I felt just like her doll as she circled me, tucking and pulling. When she instructed me, I raised and lowered my arms dutifully.

Even though I pretended to be her toy, I could feel something growing within me, something mean and ugly. No matter how hard I tried to stamp it down, it kept coming back.

I think I knew how Cinderella's stepsisters must have felt even before she married the prince. They must have envied her looks and the fact that everyone preferred Cinderella to them.

And once she had her prince, they wouldn't have wanted her gifts either because the presents would have constantly reminded them how inferior they were.

I tried to put all that in the back of my mind. First things first, though. "Mama, I need a costume. It's got to be pretty fancy because I'm going to a ball as Cinderella's stepsister."

"Boo!" Jason called. I had known that the was the way everyone was going to act when I came out on stage.

Mama sighed. "I wish you had told me earlier. I'm pretty busy."

"We should go to the fabric store and find a pattern," I said.

"We'll see," Mama said, going back to working on the blouse.

Over the next few weeks, we never got a chance because Mama began chaperoning Stephanie to various things—theater, symphony, Broadway shows, movies. And while Mama was flitting all over town with the Golden Girl, I didn't have a costume. At least Robin's grandmother was watching the kids so I could go to practice.

I thought I felt bad enough, but it got worse the night Mama told me that the Sinclairs had season's tickets to the ballet—tenth row, center orchestra.

I really felt jealous then. I had read in the paper that they had revived one of the classics in their old repertory, *Cinderella*. Madame had not been in it, but she had seen the premiere of the original. Since the choreographer was dead, they had even brought in the original dancers to teach the new dancers, both of whom I had been dying to see.

It sounded as close as I would ever get to seeing a masterpiece. And it would help so much with my own performance. It had been all that Robin, Leah and Thomas could talk about. They were going together tomorrow night to seats in nose-bleed country—high, high up in the second balcony. However, for my finances the cost of even those seats was as high as the moon.

"I hope the Sinclairs enjoy themselves," I said—though I really didn't mean it.

Mama was unpacking yet another one of our second-hand feasts. "Mr. Sinclair can't make it tomorrow night. And Miss Stephanie knows how much you love ballet—"

"How does she know that?" I asked sharply.

"She's asked me about my family," Mama said, opening a container.

"What does she care?" I asked, irritated.

Mama gave me a meaningful stare. "Miss Stephanie is interested in our family. Unlike some people in this room, she cares about others."

I could feel that ugly stepsister feeling again, but I managed to control it.

Mama emptied a container into a bowl. "At any rate, she asked if you would like to go."

This was a hard choice. Miss Stephanie might have bought Mama and my family, but not me. But miss the ballet I was dying to see? A real hard choice.

My mind immediately turned to logistics. "Who would take care of the kids?"

"I will if you want to go. Otherwise, I'll have to accompany her," Mama said. She looked puzzled when I didn't leap immediately at the chance.

"You trust me?" I asked.

"I trust you with your brothers and sisters. I assured Mr. Sinclair you were very mature. It would be almost the same as if I went," Mama said, getting out the plates. "You tell me by tomorrow morning."

I wasn't hungry so I only nibbled at dinner, leaving most of it to the kids—especially Andy—to wolf down. I got to hear more than I wanted to about Stephanie because in between mouthfuls, Mimi and Jason asked more questions about her.

What music did she play? Flute—a petite, graceful instrument. (No fat, ugly tuba for the perfect Miss Stephanie).

How many languages did she speak? Three—English, French and Chinese.

What were her favorite TV shows? None—she read for entertainment. (The last was her only demerit in Jason's book.)

And on and on through the meal until I blocked it out like traffic noise from the street. Having eaten with Stephanie already, Mama merely nibbled bits from Mimi's or Jason's plate. I caught her stealing glances at me as if I still mystified her.

I mystified myself. As soon as I could, I retreated to my room and lay down. I'd never gotten to see live ballet outside of our school performances, not even the *Nutcracker.* And Cinderella was the ballet I was going to be in.

Up till tonight, I would have dug ditches to get any ticket to the ballet, and now I was offered a free seat in the orchestra. Why didn't I jump at the chance? So what if Miss Stephanie was stuck up and full of airs? She could have been a werewolf for all I cared—just so long as I could concentrate on the ballet.

It was just this ugly, wormy feeling wriggling inside me like a giant fuzzy caterpillar.

Up until now when I read the Cinderella story, I had always sympathized with her and hated the stepsisters. Now I knew how Cinderella's stepsisters felt. Cinderella could do no wrong. They could do no right. She was beautiful. They were ugly. Everyone loved Cinderella and no one loved them.

Suddenly it hit me. In my own life story, I wasn't Cinderella. I was a stepsister.

I was jealous and angry and felt sorry for myself all at the same time. I hated whiny people who only thought about themselves. So I hated myself for being that way. I tried to talk myself out of my mood. Then I tried to scold myself out of it. Nothing worked.

I couldn't get rid of that mean and awful stepsister feeling. I could feel it growing inside me.

Maybe Madame had been right to cast me as a stepsister. It didn't help any that if I were watching myself, I would have hissed at me too.

EIGHT

The Invitation

I was still hugging my pillow when Mama came in. (She never knocked no matter how many times I had hinted that she should. Our flat was one big open barn as far as she was concerned).

My voice came muffled through the pillow. "What is it, Mama?"

Mama hovered in the doorway. "Miss Stephanie is on the telephone. She wants to know if you want the ticket."

"I don't know," I shrugged. "I've got a test coming up."

"Then I'll tell her that I'm going." Mama started to close the door.

Common sense suddenly got hold of me. "Wait!" I called.

Mama looked exasperated. "Well?"

I swallowed. "I'd like to go."

Mama smiled as if I had finally done something she

could approve of. "Miss Stephanie will be so pleased."

When she left, I rolled over flat on my back and stared at the ceiling. What was wrong with me? At this moment, I didn't even like myself. If I had to choose between Miss Stephanie or me as a friend, I would have chosen her.

When Mama barged in again, I frowned at her. "Mama—" I started to complain.

Mama ignored me as she went to my closet and opened the door. "What are you going to wear?"

"I hadn't thought about it," I said.

"Miss Stephanie has sent you so many nice things," Mama said. I heard the click of clothes hangers as she selected and then rejected items.

Great. It was bad enough I had to depend upon Stephanie's generosity to go to the ballet. Now I was going to have to dress up in her charity. What next? A sign like they have on the freeways? *This next five feet of girl taken care of by Stephanie.*

"This would look nice." Mama brought out a peach-colored, short-sleeved blouse and yellow skirt. "The weather forecaster said it's going to be warm tomorrow night so you don't want to overdress."

"Too bright," I said.

Mama turned back to my closet. I heard more clicks and then she whirled around again.

"How about this?" she asked. She had a short-sleeved blue blouse with a black skirt.

"Too tame."

Mama kept pulling out items and I kept rejecting them. However, I started to feel a little embarrassed to see how many things Stephanie had already given me, and I reminded myself to slip some of them as gifts to Leah and Robin.

Even if I couldn't see Mama's face, I could have told she was getting annoyed by all the rapid clicks from the closet.

"You have to wear something," she finally said in frustration.

I folded my arms. "Honestly. You'd think from the fuss you're making that you were the one going out with her."

"There's just no living with you anymore," Mama said in exasperation.

I threw the pillow at the floor. "Why do you always have to give me such a hard time? I'm doing the best I can."

If I'd had a camera, I could have had my mother arrested for the murderous look she gave me. "So am I. Now be a good girl."

"Why?" I asked. "What's the point? You never thank me. You only tell me what I've done wrong."

Mama shook her finger at me. "Children in America grow up too spoiled. My mother would have slapped me if I'd said that to her."

"Well, wouldn't you have liked to have your mother say something nice to you?" I asked her.

I cringed, waiting for Mama to scold me, but all she did was sit down on the bed beside me. "It's so long ago, but I guess . . . yes," she said quietly.

Mama never talked about her feelings so I was surprised when she admitted that much. The sight threw a switch in my head and tears started to come. "I'm sorry, Mama," I said, wiping my eyes on the pillow. Mama never apologized though. I'd learned at a young age that she wasn't like the American mothers on television.

"There's so much I want to do for you," Mama said. "I see all the things that Miss Stephanie has and I wish I could give them to you too."

"Really?" I asked.

"Of course," Mama said. "I'm your mother. What else would I think?"

"Well, I . . ." I felt embarrassed.

"What?" Mama demanded.

"I thought you were ashamed of me," I said in a small voice.

Mama put an arm around my shoulders. "Why? You're a good girl—most of the time."

"But you're always talking about Miss Stephanie and what she does and what she has," I said, leaning against her.

"I thought you'd want to know." Mama stroked my shoulder. "I couldn't take you to the mansion or the parties so that was my way of sharing all those wonderful things. I didn't know I was making you feel so bad. I won't do it anymore."

I gave Mama a hug. "No, keep talking. The kids certainly liked to hear them."

"But you mind," Mama protested.

"It's okay now that I know the reason," I said.

Mama began to rock me back and forth. "Things are so clear-cut in China. Here, it's all so confusing."

I hadn't thought about things from her point of view. I'd been too busy feeling sorry for myself. "It must be hard raising us," I said. "We're so Americanized."

Mama sighed. "I wish your father was here. He loved America so much. He wanted to come here. It was all he could talk about. He would have known what to do."

I sat up shyly. "I guess I'm not like those daughters on the Chinese soap operas." There were several channels in San Francisco that carried them.

"No," Mama smiled, "but then I'm not like those mothers on American television, either."

"Who says we have to be either?" I asked.

"We're us," Mama agreed.

I'd never be the obedient, uncomplaining child in the Chinese soap operas, but she'd never be the lovey-dovey mother on the American shows. I know it sounds funny, but we looked at one another as if we were really seeing each other for the first time.

With a nod, Mama got back up and went over to the closet again. "What about this blouse?" she asked, all business. She took out the white blouse she had just finished tailoring.

We settled on that with a pair of my own gray slacks.

I didn't sleep well though. I kept wondering what the real Cinderella was like. What new humiliations was the stepsister going to experience tomorrow?

NINE

An Enchanted Evening

Mama came home the next afternoon to inspect me. While she played my emergency hairdresser, she gave me a long list of things not to do. Don't be a pig. Don't impose. And dozens of other things a six-year-old might have needed to hear.

"You'd think I'd never been out of the house," I teased.

Mama grabbed my shoulder. "Don't forget to take your jacket."

"But the weather forecaster said it was going to be warm," I said. I didn't want to wear anything that bulky.

Mama got my coat out of the closet. "Put it on."

As I shrugged into it, I wondered if Mama had put a bug in it so she could monitor the whole evening.

I was glad to escape our flat. The weather forecaster had been right and Mama had been wrong. Though it was twilight, it was so warm that I almost took off my jacket, but it was hard to disobey Mama.

I followed Mama's directions to Stephanie's. It was a couple of buses away in a fancy neighborhood of San Francisco called Sea Cliff where there are multi-million dollar houses overlooking the entrance to the bay and the Golden Gate. It was getting dark by the time I got off the bus.

It's funny, but the night seemed different here. It was prettier, cleaner than at home. The sky was a sweep of black satin and the stars like bright little sequins. It even smelled different: I caught the scent of green growing things, not concrete and car exhaust.

Maybe it was the setting. The bridge arched gracefully like a slender, jeweled necklace over the dark waters. The Golden Gate must have been pretty choppy because the bay was laced with white curls and frills. I wouldn't have wanted to be in a boat down there, but up here on dry land it looked beautiful.

The houses were huge, almost like small palaces, and they had the one thing that was a real luxury in San Francisco: space for front yards. Almost all of them stood apart from their neighbors. In the other areas of San Francisco, the houses are jammed together shoulder to shoulder. I sniffed the air again and realized the smell was from freshly cut grass. They even had lawns.

The sidewalks twisted back and forth like pale lizards. As I walked along, I couldn't help marveling at how clean they looked. No dirt. No trash. No homeless asking for money.

As I passed by a brick wall, I suddenly heard a whoosh, and the breeze carried a faint mist to me. Through the iron gates, I saw that sprinklers had automatically come on on the lawn. I watched the mist rise higher and higher, swelling like some gauzy beast. As it rose toward the moon, the silvery light transformed its head into a canopy of rainbows.

I started to feel as if I were walking into the kingdom of Cinderella itself.

Suddenly in my borrowed finery, I felt like a shabby fraud. It was one thing to imagine myself among palaces. It was quite another to be in one—even if the palace had been subdivided. Had Cinderella's stepsister felt like me when she stood before the gates of Cinderella's palace?

The Sinclairs lived on the top floor of an old Victorian that had been divided into condominiums. I saw they would have a spectacular view of the bay. It was the kind of place Cinderella and her prince might rent.

Nervously I peeked through the glass door at the small foyer with half columns and marble, and the brass lights inside gleamed like gold. A plush red carpet covered the steps and even their name plates were written in a fancy calligraphic hand.

As I stood on the sidewalk, I noticed a police car

cruise slowly by, and I cringed, wanting to find some place to hide before they arrested me as a counterfeit princess. Mercifully, though, they drove on.

I almost lost my nerve. If I hadn't told my friends that I was going to the ballet, I might have turned right around and walked away before someone figured out that I didn't belong there. It felt like someone else's finger that poked the doorbell.

The next moment I heard steps from inside, and a girl swept down the steps. She was about my height with gold hair cut short like a helmet, and she walked with the grace of a born dancer. Her neck was long and as elegant as Eveline's, and I thought of how fine a line her legs and body would make when she danced.

The only odd thing was her dress. It was cut on simple lines, but it was obviously expensive. However, though it was a warm night, the sleeves were long and buttoned at the wrists. I was glad Mama had made me wear the blouse with the short sleeves.

"Hello," her voice came faintly from inside. "Are you Amy?"

"Yes," I said. "And you're Stephanie?"

As she nodded, her eyes took in the blouse as she unlocked the door. "That blouse looks good on you."

"Yes, thank you," I said stroking the lacy collar self-consciously.

She motioned up the stairs. "Would you like to come up? I just called a taxi."

I'd never ridden in a taxi. "I thought we were taking the bus," I blurted out.

Stephanie seemed disturbed. "Would you rather take a bus? I'll cancel the taxi." At that moment, a bright yellow taxi pulled up in front of her place. "Oh, dear. There must have been one in the neighborhood. Do you want to tell him to go away?"

I shrugged. "Since he's here. . ."

As the cabby started to get out of his taxi, Stephanie raised a hand. "We'll be out in a minute," she called to him.

With a nod, he got back inside.

"I've got to get my purse. I'll be right down," she assured me, and then scampered back up the steps.

As I stood there, I noticed that the marble wasn't real but had been painted to look like marble. I bent down to examine it. It was good enough to fool the eye from a few feet away. It made me wonder how much was real inside the palace.

"Are you all right?" Stephanie asked from up above.

I straightened hurriedly and saw her standing upon the stairs. She had put on a coat and had a slender white purse in one hand. "Yes, I thought I lost a penny." Immediately I scolded myself for not making it a dollar. I sounded like a cheap skate. "It's my lucky penny," I improvised.

Stephanie skipped down the steps and started to look. "Then we must find it." She was so eager to please.

My cheeks reddening, I stopped her. "We should go outside. The cab's waiting."

"Yes, well, I'll look when I come back, and if I can't find it, I'll put up a notice," Stephanie promised.

I didn't see any reason to advertise my stupidity. "It's okay," I said.

"No," she said firmly. "You don't squander luck."

"Aren't you warm?" I asked, trying to change the subject.

"I saw the fog blowing in through the Golden Gate," Stephanie said as she opened the door.

The breeze was blowing wisps of fog down the street as if there were a parade of ghosts. Because San Francisco was on a peninsula, the series of bays inland drew in the wind and fog from the ocean. When San Francisco's "air conditioner" had kicked in, the Richmond district was always the first to feel it. So Mama had been right after all to make me take a jacket.

The cab had that new car smell as if it had just rolled out of the factory, and we slid onto the brown vinyl seats. I wanted to look like I took taxis every day so I tried hard not to stare.

Stephanie leaned forward to talk through the narrow opening in the protective glass separating the cabby from the passengers. "War Memorial Opera House please."

As the taxi took off, I asked her the usual polite questions: How did she like San Francisco? How did she like her tutors?

She answered me in a friendly, brief manner, but she seemed more interested in me and my family. It surprised me how much she already knew, and I tried to reply. But most of my mind was occupied with the taxi meter where the numbers kept rising alarmingly. Even if Stephanie was going to pay, it seemed like a shameful waste of money.

I was so distracted by her questions and the meter that I didn't notice when we got to the War Memorial Opera House.

"Let me get this," she said quickly, snapping open her purse. I hadn't even thought of the possibility of my having to pay. Uneasily I began to wonder how much money I had on me.

I had often passed by the War Memorial Opera House on the way to the Main Library, and in the daylight it had been just another public building, squat and massive.

Now I was seeing it in its proper setting—with an excited audience moving in a dark carpet up the steps. Most of the men were in suits and a few were even in tuxedos. The women were dressed in everything from business suits to fancy dresses.

Once inside the lobby, everyone began to flow to the left and right in two great rivers, moving toward the stairs and the elevators.

That left a smaller stream pouring toward the orchestra seats. Here were the men in the tuxes and women in evening outfits straight out of the evening pages of *Vogue*. I even saw one woman in a small turban with a peacock feather and filmy harem pants. Since Stephanie didn't stare, I tried not to. I wanted to act as if I did this every week, but my eyes kept darting to the left and the right.

We were carried on a surge of the crowd through the doors. And the opera house just seemed to open up like a huge golden cavern. Ali Baba must have felt the same awe when he stepped into the cave of the forty thieves and saw the glow of the precious treasure.

"Tickets?" an elderly woman asked. She was dressed in black with a white collar and had a handful of programs fanned out in her fingers like a poker hand.

"Well, I . . ." I looked all around for Stephanie.

Before I could panic though, Stephanie ran toward me. "There you are," she said. Behind her she had her own usher dressed in dark blue.

"Excuse me," I said to the other usher and followed Stephanie and her guide down to the tenth row in the center of the orchestra. Handing us programs, she pointed out our seats and we made our way over to them.

As I started to unzip my jacket, I felt a tug at my collar. It took me a moment to realize Stephanie was helping me out of my coat. I couldn't remember ever having anyone do that. "Thanks," I mumbled self-consciously. Then I draped my jacket against the back of my seat and then returned the favor.

Some of the musicians had already sat down. The

curtain was still drawn, but lights lit up the folds, accenting the shadows. As I gazed at the stage, I could feel my excitement growing.

For a moment I imagined that it was my name in the program, and that all these people had come to see me on stage. I could imagine being on the other side of the curtain, standing on the wings, in costume and make-up, waiting for that moment when I would spring out, and the lights would hit me.

Stephanie took my arm. "One of these days I'll be watching you up there."

I found myself blushing. How had she guessed what was on my mind? "I don't ever expect to be up there on that stage," I mumbled.

"Nonsense. Your mother says you're a wonderful dancer," Stephanie said. "One of these days I hope to see one of your recitals."

I thought of our little ballet school auditorium. The music was on compact disk, the lights few, and the chorus made up of beginners.

"It's nothing like this," I said humbly.

"But imagine seeing a prima ballerina at the beginning of her career," Stephanie said.

I hadn't thought of it that way.

She leaned in closer. "Tell me, Amy. What does a ballerina do to remember her own performance? Have someone videotape her?"

I had seen videotapes of my own performances.

"You can only see a videotape on a flat television screen. It's not the same as seeing it live on stage."

Suddenly the conductor appeared by the podium, bowing to the audience as we applauded, and then turned back to the orchestra and raised his baton.

Sweet music rose from the orchestra pit, swelling until it filled the whole opera house. We were so close that I could feel the music vibrating under my skin.

Stephanie snapped her purse open. "Here. I brought a pair of opera glasses," she said, holding up a small, dainty pair of binoculars.

I was beginning to feel I had been wrong about Stephanie. I had been expecting some spoiled brat. Instead I found someone sweet and thoughtful. Why did Cinderella have to be so nice? It didn't help any that Mama had been right about her after all.

Feeling guilty, I took them as the curtain began to rise and the first act began.

The dancing was wonderful, far better than anything I could ever hope to do. Legs lifted longer and jumped higher. Bodies slanted in elegant lines. No one forgot their steps. I couldn't help thinking that Eveline was ready to join the dancers on stage.

Our seats were wonderful to see their technique. We were so close to the dancers that I could even see them perspire. They were all so lovely and graceful that it's easy to forget a ballet performance is as athletic as a basketball game.

When the first act was done, I balanced the program and opera glasses on my lap so I could clap. Then, as the music began again, I realized I'd had the opera glasses the whole time.

"I'm sorry. I didn't mean to hog these." I tried to give the opera glasses back to Stephanie, but she pushed them away with her program.

"I brought them for you to enjoy," she said.

"That's very thoughtful," I said, surprised. "Thank you." I was beginning to feel even more guilty.

Could a stepsister make up with Cinderella?

I decided I was going to try.

TEN

Guilt Trip

At intermission, we joined the flow of people moving into the lobby and then got in line with the other women before the women's restrooms.

"So what does a real ballerina like you think of the performance?" Stephanie asked.

Since it was the only live performance I had seen, I could truthfully say, "It's the best I ever saw." I didn't want to admit to someone like Stephanie that this was my first live ballet.

"Don't you think Mimi would have liked the costumes?" she asked.

"Yes, she would," I agreed.

Stephanie chuckled, "And Jason would have liked that dancer with the big nose. He was so funny."

"Amy." Madame lined up behind us. "It is good to see the ballet here first." She had been encouraging all of us to see *Cinderella* before our own performance.

"Madame." I almost curtsied. Usually she was dressed in sensible wool cardigans, but tonight she was in a filmy rose-colored dress with broad shoulders and puffy sleeves.

Madame was glowing from the memory of the first half of the ballet. "They are very fine." I felt reassured by her judgment.

"I didn't know you were going to be here," I said.

"I stand in the second balcony." Madame indicated the huge binoculars hanging from her neck. The binoculars looked as big as cannons and I wondered how she could keep her head up, let alone hold them up for a whole evening.

I remembered my manners and introduced Madame to Stephanie.

After nodding to Stephanie, Madame folded her hands and turned back to me. "And what do you think, Amy?"

"I think it's magical," I said.

"Magical," Madame almost chewed the word and then smiled. "That is a good word. *Cinderella* is about magic."

"I thought it was about an underdog getting her reward," I said, puzzled. "Oh, you mean the fairy godmother and the pumpkin and the gown and stuff."

Madame shook her head. "Forget the cartoon. It is not about looking pretty and getting all the attention. Cinderella makes herself all over again. That is magic."

Stephanie was quicker than me. "Ah," she said, lifting her head. "That's why this ballerina does more than put on the new gown. She changes her attitude."

Madame took on an aristocratic pose with all her years of performing. "Just so. She becomes a princess, not a girl playing dress up."

"She becomes what she wants to be," I said thoughtfully. Finally I understood how Madame was directing Eveline, who was dancing the role of Cinderella.

Stephanie tapped a finger to her lips. "I saw a production in Copenhagen where the ballerina danced it just the same way."

As it turned out, she had seen productions in London and Vienna as well. And she had asked *me* what my opinion was. I should have been asking *hers*.

And that's what really struck me as odd. Instead of discussing the other ballet companies, she had discussed my family. From the moment we had gotten into the taxi, she had talked about my family.

Maybe she was just trying to be polite, but it almost seemed as if she didn't have a life of her own.

When it was finally my turn, I got into the stall and opened my purse. I didn't really have to go. I just wanted to see how much cash I had. I still had a few dollars from my last baby-sitting job. Fortunately, I also had my birthday money in my wallet. I had enough to get Stephanie home and then myself. I wasn't going to have her treat to the whole evening.

When I got back outside, I kept Madame company while Stephanie went in. "And did you see what the stepsisters did in contrast to Cinderella?" Madame asked.

"I haven't been watching them that much," I confessed.

"You watch them too," Madame told me. "They are very important."

I thought Madame was just trying to make me feel good about being cast as a stepsister. "I guess the audience needs someone mean to hiss at."

Madame frowned as she always did when I made a mistake. "No, no, they are not mean."

"But they do all those nasty things to Cinderella," I said.

Madame wagged her head from side to side. "Yes, well, they are not mean for the sake of being cruel. They do those things because they believe people like them should always be on top and people like Cinderella should always be on the bottom."

"That's why they're so terrible to the beggar woman in the first act," I said. The beggar woman had been the fairy godmother in disguise. I was beginning to get a glimmering of how to play my role. They would go to the ball as was their due—to mix with their own kind. The joke on them was that they weren't.

Madame beamed. "Just so. They are the opposite of Cinderella. If Cinderella is open to change, they hate it. They want everything to stay the same."

That hit home. "What's wrong with that?" I asked.

Madame pressed her palms together almost as if in prayer. "They are like barnacles, all closed up to the world—to people—and that makes them all closed up to magic."

I wasn't like that. I was open to people . . . sort of. I started thinking over the recent past and didn't feel that certain. I hadn't been very friendly toward Stephanie.

Worse, I had been as selfish as one of Cinderella's stepsisters, wanting my life to go the way it had before Mama had become an amah. That was because my life, even if I had to worry about money, had still been pretty comfortable. But how comfortable was life for Mama?

"But what if the change means the stepsisters have to give up something they love?" I asked Madame.

Then Madame studied me as if she were putting two and two together—my absences and my excuses. "Does this change really mean the stepsister must give up what she loves?"

Since Robin's grandmother didn't seem to mind baby-sitting the brats, I could make class. As long as Mama was an amah, we had the money, so I could keep on learning from Madame. "No," I admitted, "the stepsister wouldn't have to give it up. Not totally."

"Then," Madame said, "she can not complain about change, can she?"

"No," I said, feeling a little better.

Madame was as wise as Robin's grandmother. I

almost did a reverence right there in the restroom line. I satisfied myself with a heartfelt, "Thank you."

I was so pleased to have this chance to talk with her that I hadn't even noticed that Stephanie had come out again. "Your turn," she said to Madame.

Just at that moment, the lights began to flash, and the other women waiting in line gave a groan.

"I'm sorry, Madame," I said. "I should have let you go first."

"Ballet is not for sissies," Madame sniffed. Then, with a nod to us, she began to jog back to her standing place in the balcony before someone else could take it.

During the second act, I kept an eye on the stepsisters in the ball at the prince's castle. And I could see what Madame meant. They thought they were as good as the courtiers, but they were always a little off. Sometimes it was their position. Sometimes they danced too fast or too slow.

Even their mouths were pressed into thin, tight lines as if they were sealed as tight as a tin can. They were shut off from people and magic.

The dancing itself in this act and the third was even better than in the first. Long after the curtain had dropped, I stared at the stage, not wanting it to end. I kept clapping all the while. Then I turned to Stephanie. "Thank you."

"I'm glad you enjoyed it," she said.

I handed her the opera glasses. "So you go to the ballet a lot?"

"Father likes us to enjoy the culture that a city offers," she said.

"How many places have you lived anyway?" I asked.

"We lived mostly in Hong Kong, but we've stayed for periods of time in eight cities that I remember," Stephanie said.

I twisted around and looked up in the balcony. "I don't see Madame."

"Perhaps she went to refresh herself," Stephanie said. She was full of quaint euphemisms—as if I were talking to Jane Austen.

"Why don't we give your teacher a lift home too?" Stephanie suggested.

I didn't stop to think about what that might mean. "Would you mind?"

"Not in the least," Stephanie said, rising.

We helped one another into our coats and then joined the tail end of the crowd as it trickled slowly out of the theater. We caught Madame just as she was coming out of the restroom.

"Wasn't it wonderful?" she asked, her eyes shining.

It was nice to have an experience like this to share with Madame. "I don't think I'll ever forget it."

"I saw you down below," Madame said.

"I hope we weren't doing anything embarrassing," Stephanie laughed.

Madame had many virtues, but a sense of humor was not one of them. She took everything seriously. "No, you were quite well-behaved."

"Can we take you home?" Stephanie asked.

I was eager to do something nice for my teacher. "It would be on our way home."

"Well, I would be most grateful," Madame said.

Outside, though, there were nearly a dozen well-dressed couples competing for taxis, and two pairs were arguing over the one available cab. "It will be a while. I hope it will be all right," Stephanie apologized to Madame.

"I was expecting to take a bus so time does not matter to me, but you children should be in bed," Madame muttered, then pivoted.

I turned with her. Between the opera house and the Veteran's Auditorium was an oval stretch of lawn. I saw a couple of limousines parked there.

Madame pointed to the next block. "I see taxis on Franklin. Come. We will intercept."

Madame led us across the block to Franklin and strode right to the curb. Raising her hand, she called in a voice that had been commanding thousands of children to stand up on their toes, "Taxi!"

Immediately a cab screeched to a halt as the cars behind it hit their brakes and horns.

As if she did this all the time, Madame opened the passenger door and waved to us. "Come."

"Merci," Stephanie said.

Madame murmured something in French as she got in behind us. For about a mile, I was completely out of it as they spoke French.

Finally Madame studied Stephanie's slender frame and then patted Stephanie on the arm. "You should think of taking up ballet yourself. You have an elegant line."

For a moment, I felt a twinge of jealousy, but I fought it down. The stepsister was going to stay dead and buried.

"No, I leave that to Amy," Stephanie said, glancing at me.

Madame lived in an apartment near her school. "That is it," Madame said, pointing as we passed her school. "It is small, but many of our dancers go on to join professional companies. And the ones who don't will be graceful all their lives."

Stephanie leaned over in the seat, trying to see it better. "It would be nice to be graceful."

"Come for lessons," Madame urged her. "Now you know where it is."

It was only when we had left off Madame that I realized my mistake. "Now what's your address?" Stephanie asked.

I checked the meter. Originally I had planned to take Stephanie home first and then have the cab head to our area. I thought of giving her all my money, but it seemed a little tacky to pull out quarters and dimes as well as crumpled dollar bills.

I was also wondering what she would make of my home. It wasn't that I was ashamed of where I lived, but it didn't match any of the places I had seen in Sea Cliff.

"No, this is my treat. Let's take you home first," I said hastily.

"It makes more sense to drop you off next," she said.

"I can afford it," I bristled.

She backtracked hastily. "Of course you can. I just meant that since I had invited you, I had expected to pay for all the expenses."

"I can't be totally in your debt," I insisted.

She squirmed uncomfortably. "Please."

"No, let me. I mean it," I said.

She sank back against the seat as if trapped. "Well, then, thank you."

I gave her address to the cabby and the taxi shot forward. Stephanie watched the Chinese restaurants and vegetable stores pass by. They were calling the Richmond district the New Chinatown nowadays.

She stared out the window the whole time, and despite myself, I began to feel ashamed. Everything must seem so shabby compared to her palace.

At her house, Stephanie got out of the taxi. "Thank you so much for the lift."

"Well, thank you for the evening. I won't ever forget it," I said.

"And I'm so looking forward to staying with you," Stephanie said.

"Staying?" I asked.

"Yes, didn't your mother tell you?" Stephanie asked.

"No," I said, feeling numb inside.

"While my father's away on business for the next few weeks, I'm going to stay with you," Stephanie said. "Won't that be fun?"

I would find out soon enough what the princess thought of my home.

Stephanie seemed to be waiting for some reply.

"Yeah, fun," I said dumbly. Just when I was getting to like her, Stephanie kept throwing more curve balls at me.

As she shut the door, the cabby asked, "Where to?"

I glanced at the meter. I still had a little leeway. "Wait. Let's make sure she gets in okay."

"Suit yourself," the cabby said.

I watched Stephanie walk briskly up toward her door, opening her purse as she went. Fishing out her keys, she slipped into her house and waved as she closed the door again.

The numbers on the meter changed.

"Just around the corner," I said.

The cabby roared off and around the corner, screeching to a halt.

Now that we were out of sight, I counted out all my money and gave it to him. "There's fifty cents for you too. Sorry."

"Great. I'm halfway to a cup of coffee," he said sarcastically.

I wish I could have told him how long I had worked

to earn that much, but I just got out of the taxi. He raced away as if he couldn't wait to escape girls with pretensions of being rich.

Zipping up my jacket, I got ready for a three-mile walk back home. This time of night there wouldn't be many buses. It was okay though. I was furious at my mother. I had a lot of energy to walk off.

ELEVEN

Grandmother

I got up early the next morning and sat in the hallway so I could pounce on my mother as soon as she came out of her bedroom. Most parents, when they saw their daughter, would have asked if the daughter'd had fun, but my mother's first question was, "Did you behave yourself last night?"

I planted myself between her and the bathroom so that she had to face me. "What's the big idea?" I demanded. "When we're you going to tell me Stephanie was going to stay with us? When you asked me to help her with her bags?" She'd probably have a trunk-load for all her clothes.

Mama blinked her eyes innocently. "I was meaning to talk with you about that. I think you should give the whole house a good cleaning. It really needs it. We can't have Miss Stephanie think we live like pigs."

I slapped my sides in frustration. "When do I have the time?"

"When you watch your brothers and sisters, of course," Mama said.

"And when do I do my homework and do my ballet?" I demanded.

"Well, what time do I have?" Mama asked self-righteously. "I'm too busy working."

I just stared at Mama. "Yeah, it must be rough having tea and eating big dinners all the time."

"It's harder than you think." Mama looked like she wanted to say more but instead she pressed her lips together tightly.

"How?" I asked skeptically. Her descriptions to us made it sound like paradise.

Mama lifted her head as if she were about to scold me but caught herself. I think she was remembering our talk from the other night so she at least made an effort to explain. "I didn't have any choice about inviting Miss Stephanie. Mr. Sinclair got an urgent call. He has to leave town almost immediately, and he needed to have someone stay with Stephanie. But I asked the Sinclairs if Stephanie could move in with us because . . ." She broke off suddenly embarrassed.

"Because why?" I prompted her.

"I wanted to be with you and your brothers and sisters," Mama said.

"You don't act like it," I said.

"Do you think I like leaving you every day?" Mama asked. "These are precious years. I want to be with you.

It makes me feel guilty to go away." She looked ready to cry.

I realized I'd been selfish again. "I'm sorry, Mama."

"Besides," she smiled, "this way we don't have to ask Robin's grandmother to watch them."

"You mean I have to baby-sit them as well as Miss Stephanie?" I asked in exasperation.

"No, I'll watch your brothers and sisters," Mama said. "You're just supposed to keep Miss Stephanie company."

"But I can go to practice." When Mama nodded, I sighed. "All right. How long do I have?"

"I think she's coming Friday," Mama said. "I'll check tonight."

"Friday. That's only one day away," I said in a daze.

"I told you that the trip came up suddenly," Mama said. "I'll do what I can when I come back from Miss Stephanie's. Between the two of us, we should manage."

A new question popped up into my head. "Where she's going to sleep?" I asked.

"Well, she can hardly sleep with Jason and Andy," Mama hurried toward the bathroom. "Mimi and Didi can move in with me."

I shared a room with my sisters. "So Stephanie can sleep in one of the girls' bunks?"

Mama was scandalized. "Of course not. We'll give her your bed. You can't expect Miss Stephanie to sleep on a narrow, little bunk bed."

No, that was only for a mean, old, ugly stepsister like me. All the dark feelings came wriggling back—like a furry caterpillar writhing around and making me itch maddeningly.

Mama opened the door to the bathroom. "Please, Amy. Don't give me that look. You should be grateful that Miss Stephanie was thrilled to visit us."

"Great," I muttered to the door. "Not only do I have to sleep on the girls' beds and clean the house, but I have to like it too."

I don't remember much of the day. I was too busy storming around with a telephone-pole-sized chip on my shoulder. I was so angry I even missed my cues during practice. At the end, Madame gave a lecture to the class on focus, but I knew the words were meant for me.

On our way to her grandmother's to pick up my brothers and sisters, Robin asked me, "Where were you today, Amy? Your body was out there, but your brain was on Mars."

I didn't know where to start. How could you complain about someone being too perfect? Or having that person be nice to you? Even to my own ears, I sounded like a whiner.

"Just stuff," I shrugged.

Robin studied me a moment and then shifted her bag to her other shoulder. "Well, when you want to talk about that 'stuff,' just call me."

I was glad to have a friend like Robin. "Yeah," I said, and added, "thanks."

Robin's grandmother lived in a little apartment beneath the house of one of her sons. Even before we knocked, we could hear loud thumps and then a bugle playing victory. "That sound must be driving your grandmother crazy by now."

It was so loud, it was a wonder that anyone heard Robin's knock, but her grandmother yelled over the bugle, "It's open."

When we stepped inside the dark apartment, we saw that a video game had been hooked up to the television. On the screen, wolf warriors were strutting about victoriously and Jason, Andy, Mimi, Didi and Robin's brother Ian were giving each other high-fives.

Grandmother was sitting on the floor with her legs crossed and a control stick in her hand. "Come in and play," she called to us, holding up the controls. She had a slight British accent like Mama that she had also picked up in Hong Kong.

"She's at level five," Jason said, awed. "I've never made it past three." That was the ultimate compliment from him.

Grandmother pushed a button and the game swung into the next level. "I should have borrowed this a long time ago from my son's store. I didn't know what fun they were." She hunched forward, intent on wiping out the bad guys.

Grandmother squirmed over to make room for us. "Come on, Amy. You take a turn."

All I wanted to do was just snuggle up against her

comfortable shape. I wanted her to make everything all right.

At any other time, I would have been happy to play and forget my troubles, but today all I could think about was Mama's chores. There was no escaping Cinderella-Stephanie.

"No thanks," I said reluctantly. "We should be leaving soon." As the brats started to complain, I snapped, "Quiet. We've got homework and chores."

Grandmother studied me and then held up the controls to Robin. "You play for me," she said.

As Robin sat down, the kids scooted over eagerly to coach her. Grandmother twisted around and put a hand on the sofa to help her stand up. "Amy can help me get some snacks together." She looked up at me. "You have time for snacks, don't you?"

It was hard to refuse a crippled lady. "Sure," I said, handing her canes to her. "Thanks for taking care of my family. I hope they haven't been too much trouble."

"They've been angels," Grandmother said, beaming at them.

I found that hard to believe, but I didn't say so. "By the way, my mother will be able to take care of them next week."

Grandmother seemed disappointed. "What a shame."

Her kitchenette was hardly big enough for her, let

alone me, but I managed to squeeze in behind her. There was a half-refrigerator on the floor with a sink and two burners above it. And hanging over that was an oven.

"Would you put some water on?" she asked, nodding toward the kettle on the stove. It was like being on a crowded bus as we brushed past each other. While I filled the kettle, she got a box of tea from one cabinet and then a bag of Japanese rice crackers from another.

When the water was heating on the stove, she opened the package of crackers. "Now why don't you tell me what's bothering you?" she asked in Chinese. The kids didn't speak it well. We could have some privacy talking in Chinese.

"Nothing, really," I said, turning on the gas jet.

"I think of you almost like another granddaughter," she said, arranging the crackers on a plate. "So don't tell me that."

I had never known my own grandmother. She'd stayed behind in Hong Kong when my parents came over, and she had died shortly after I was born here. Sometimes I liked to pretend that Robin's grandmother was mine—she often acted like it. So it made me feel warm inside to hear that.

"And I think of you like a grandmother," I said.

She folded her hands in front of her. "All right then, what's wrong? You're always so cheerful. Now you're a regular little storm cloud."

Suddenly I couldn't keep it back any longer. "Well, I've been having to handle more of the chores at home since my mother's took this job. I guess I'm getting worn down."

"And you'd like more time for yourself?" Grandmother asked.

"Well, that would be nice, but that's not really it." I folded my arms. "I'd settle for a thank you."

Grandmother arched her eyebrows. "You don't think your mother appreciates you. Right?"

I thought of this morning. "I do everything I can, and yet she just wants more."

Grandmother took a battered old tea ball from a drawer. It was covered with tiny holes like a strainer and she unscrewed the halves. "Your mother's old-fashioned. So was I until I came here. When I was in Hong Kong, I never praised Robin's mother. There's a proverb in Chinese that says something like 'Praise the child, spoil the child.' "

"But you're not like that with Robin and Ian," I said.

Grandmother opened a tin of tea. "Grandmothers are never as hard on their grandchildren as they were on their children."

"But my mother can be nice to other children." I could hear the frustration in my own voice. I told her about how much my mother admired Stephanie and how she wanted me to prepare for her visit.

"Remember, Stephanie is not her daughter." Grandmother began to pack tea into the ball. "America is a hard place. Some people get scared for their own children so they cling even harder to the old ways."

"But we have trouble talking together," I said.

Grandmother screwed the halves of the tea ball shut again. "That doesn't mean she doesn't love you. Chinese mothers show their love in deeds, not in words."

I thought about it. There had been times this last year when Mama had dropped hints that I might have to give up lessons, but when she saw how upset I had been, she had always found the money somehow.

"I guess so," I said.

The kettle started to whistle, but I just stared at it. I was thinking over what Madame had said about the stepsisters who were shut up tight like barnacles. That was my mother to a "T." "I don't think Mama will ever change."

Grandmother put the tea ball into a tea pot. There was a chain at the top of the tea ball with a hook and she used it to hang onto the opening at the top of the pot. "I know it's hard, but try to be patient. Mothers can do worse things in the name of love."

"Like what?" I asked, continuing to watch the kettle boil.

Grandmother stretched past me to turn it off and lowered her voice. "You have to promise not to tell anyone what I'm going to tell you."

I was suddenly curious. "I promise."

"Have you ever wondered what happened to my feet?" she asked, gesturing to her feet with a cane.

"Sure," I admitted reluctantly. "I always figured your feet got hurt in some accident."

"I told Robin not to tell anyone," Grandmother said.

I could tell she was sensitive about it. "Wild horses couldn't drag it out of me," I said.

"My mother bound my feet," Grandmother whispered.

"I've heard about that," I said, "but what is that exactly?"

Grandmother leaned against a counter. "My mother slowly bent my toes under the soles of my feet. I was in pain for several years."

It made my skin crawl. "How could she do that to you?"

Grandmother motioned me to lower my voice. "She thought it would make me lovely. Then I could marry a rich man."

"That's awful," I said. I don't know what I would have done if I couldn't dance.

Grandmother shrugged. "Yes, but she didn't do it to be mean. She really believed she was making me beautiful."

My own feet ached in sympathy. "Why would she think that?"

"Because at one time, some Chinese thought it made women look beautiful," Grandmother said. "In Europe and America, small waists used to be the rage. Women even had ribs removed so they could be slender, and every proper woman used a corset. They were bound so tight that women used to faint and it led to all sorts of health problems."

"But that's not as bad as binding the feet," I said. It gave me a creepy feeling. "I'm sorry." I almost wish she hadn't told me.

I rubbed my own feet together to reassure myself. "Do they hurt still?"

"Yes, but that's because I took off the bindings," Grandmother said. "You learn to live with the pain."

I hugged her. "I'm so sorry."

She squeezed me back. "I would never have told you about it, but I wanted you to understand that there are worse things that mothers can do to daughters."

It made my mother seem harmless in comparison. "And I won't tell anyone."

"You'd better not," Grandmother said. "Now help me find the tray."

TWELVE

The Cinderella Effect

I needed every word of encouragement. Princess Cinderella was coming. After the night of the ballet, I liked Stephanie, though I still found her a little odd. So I didn't blame her personally for making me slave away getting the flat ready. If she had known how much trouble this visit would cause, I don't think she would have come.

As soon as we got home, I started on my list of chores, but it seemed like every time I tidied up a space, the kids made it dirty again.

Finally I just blew up at them. "If you don't leave this room like you found it, I'm . . . I'm going to lock you in a closet."

Mimi's eyes grew real big. "You wouldn't." She hesitated and added, "Would you?"

Jason was more of a rebel. He screwed up his face angrily. "Go ahead. I'll tell Mama. I'll tell my teacher. I'll tell the police. They'll take you to jail."

Didi and Andy just started crying.

I felt like a real monster then. I thought of how much interest Stephanie took in my family. I should have tried to appreciate them myself. "Look. Let's start over again. Mama wants this place to be neat for Miss Stephanie. If you keep messing it up, Mama won't let her come."

That threat worked. "Oh," Jason said and looked at Mimi.

"We'll straighten up after ourselves," Mimi promised and Jason nodded solemnly.

I suppose I should have been glad for any kind of cooperation, but it was as if they loved Miss Stephanie more than they did me.

It was that Cinderella effect all over again. They weren't afraid of the evil stepsister dropping dead from overwork, but heaven forbid that they should disappoint Cinderella. But how could I hate her when she was so nice?

"Quit whining," I muttered to myself and went to take care of the next chore.

Mama helped as soon as she got home. The trouble was that she kept coming up with a new chores. There always seemed to be something new to dust, wash and clean.

When Mama finally decided our place was clean, the real torture started. Mama took me to my closet to pick out an outfit. "You don't want her to think we're beggars," she said.

"We're going to be sharing the same room," I said. "There aren't going to be any secrets about my closet."

"We want to start this visit off on the right foot," Mama insisted.

I wound up having to set out my dress-up clothes for the next day.

On Friday I had to keep reminding myself about what Robin's grandmother had told me. And in the afternoon when I picked up the children, she gave me another pep talk.

At home, I got the kids into their good clothes and then put on my own. I had just finished when the taxi brought Mama and Miss Stephanie.

I waited for the cabby to haul out a trunkload of suitcases, but all she had was a single suitcase and a shopping bag.

If she was shocked by our place, she didn't show it. Instead she set down her things and held out her arms. The kids swarmed all over her. I'd never gotten that kind of welcome no matter how much I had done for them.

Of course, the shopping bag had nothing but more presents. More comic books for the kids. Mama had a bouquet of flowers.

Mama laid them on the table. "Look what Miss Stephanie bought me. Roses. My favorite."

If Mama had been Pinocchio, her nose would have

been a block long by now. This was the first I ever heard her say she liked roses.

"And I hope you like this, Amy," Stephanie handed me a compact disc. "It's the music to Prokofiev's *Cinderella*."

"You remembered," I said, beginning to feel a little of the Cinderella effect myself.

Mama nudged me impatiently. "What do you say?"

"Uh . . . thanks," I said.

Stephanie smiled at all of us. "I've been looking forward to this."

"So have we," Mama said, and elbowed me again. "Amy, show Miss Stephanie to your room."

"I hope I'm not being any trouble." Stephanie said and started to take her suitcase, but Mama picked it up and handed it to me.

"Oh, no. No trouble at all," Mama beamed.

The suitcase wasn't all that heavy. I led Stephanie down to the hallway and opened my door. You could actually see the floor now, and all our books and stuff were up on shelves for the first time.

"You can have my bed," I said, indicating the freshly changed, freshly made-up bed.

Stephanie hesitated in the doorway. "I can sleep on one of the bunk beds." She nodded to where Mimi and Didi slept.

"Don't be silly," Mama said. Taking her elbow, she guided Stephanie into my room.

I felt as if my room were being invaded.

Miss Stephanie looked uncomfortable. "I was expecting to sleep on a sofa," she said.

Mama patted her arm. "We couldn't have that. What would your father think?"

"Really, it's fine," I lied.

Mama was cheerful now that I had said and done the proper thing. "So you go off to your practice now."

I changed and went to practice. I wasn't aching in such odd places anymore. I guess I was getting used to my role.

When I got back home, everybody was laughing as if it was a real party. I showered and changed back into my good clothes.

As soon as I walked into the living room, Mama turned to Stephanie. "So what would you like to eat tonight?"

"Well, why don't we order a pizza?" Stephanie said.

Mama had been cutting up food all day in preparation for a home-cooked Chinese meal. "But Mama—" I began to tell her.

However, Mama cut in quickly. "Yes, but it's my treat. You're our guest."

Stephanie and Mama argued for a little bit—that part reminded me of a Chinese meal where everyone wants to pick up the check—but eventually Stephanie gave in. Of course, the kids all wanted different toppings on the pizza.

I was going to tell them to order a pizza with every-thing like we always did, but Stephanie suggested, "Why don't we order four?"

I think Mama did a mental gulp over our finances, but smiled bravely. "Good idea," she said.

When Stephanie started to set the table, I noticed how quickly my brothers and sisters jumped to help her. No pouting. No screaming. No pleading. No threats. They were truly under Cinderella's spell.

When the pizzas arrived, Mama wouldn't allow us to eat them right away. "Wait, wait." She hurried into the kitchen, and a moment later I heard her calling to me. "Amy, where's the teapot?"

"On the bottom shelf," I said. I was terribly hungry smelling the pizza.

A moment later, Mama shouted. "No, not that one. The special teapot."

That gave me a start. Now I knew how much Mama treasured Miss Stephanie. She had never brought the teapot out for my friends.

"Coming," I said, and went into the kitchen.

"Miss Stephanie's used to nice things," Mama ex-plained before I could ask.

I got on my knees and got the teapot out of the cab-inet where we had placed it after our tea with Auntie Ruby. "Every time you use it, you run a risk."

"Only you or I will pour, and only you or I will clean it," Mama said. "Is that understood?"

Great. All I needed was another job. All to impress Stephanie. No, it wasn't to impress. It was just to make her feel "at home" because we had expensive things too.

I was going to pour the boiling water into the teapot, but Mama stopped me. "We have to put hot water in it first."

I didn't see the point though. "It's clean," I said, "and it can't be dusty because we just used it."

Mama clicked her tongue in exasperation. "We absolutely must warm the pot first."

I was exasperated by all the chores Mama came up with. "Why?"

Mama swirled the hot water around inside the teapot. "Don't ask so many questions and get the tea."

I waited impatiently while she went through the whole ritual. We always had to do things Mama's way.

"Oh, how lovely," Stephanie said when Mama brought out the tea.

"I knew you'd appreciate it," Mama said, pleased.

"We have a teapot just like it at home," Stephanie said.

"Really?" Mama asked surprised. "I've never seen it."

"It was my mother's," Stephanie said. "Father has it stored away."

"A wise choice," Mama said approvingly.

"I want soda," Jason pouted.

"Me too," Didi said. Mimi and Andy joined in.

"You know where they are. Get 'em," I growled.

Mama frowned at me for slipping out of my lady-like role, then turned to Stephanie.

"Tea?" she asked.

"Please," Stephanie said.

I only drank one cup of tea myself. I knew that the less Mama picked up the teapot, the less risk we ran. I definitely was going to let Mama clean it.

When Andy started to reach for the teapot, Mama cleared her throat pointedly. "You still have soda to drink."

Andy snatched his hand back. "I just wanted to pet the dragon."

"He looks like a lonely dragon. I think he wants some attention," Stephanie said and, reaching out her hand, she stroked its back. "Nice dragon," she said as if talking to a cat.

With a triumphant grin, Andy stretched out his fingers. "Nice dragon," he said, but when he saw Mama's dark look, he only petted it once.

Afterwards, there was a game of Monopoly which Stephanie won. I'd never seen Mama enjoy herself so much. She was always smiling and laughing. She hardly ever did that when she was around me. It made me wonder what was wrong with me.

The only hitch in the evening was when our guest suddenly got up and headed for the kitchen. Mama gave me an urgent poke. "See what Miss Stephanie wants. Whatever you do, don't let her look into the refrigerator."

So I got up to follow her. "What would you like?" I asked her.

"I felt like some juice," she said. "I can help myself." She was already opening up the refrigerator door. She stopped, though, when she saw all the containers. "Look at all this food."

I thought quickly. "Mama got it ready for tomorrow night."

Stephanie wasn't stupid though. "She was going to cook tonight, wasn't she?" When I didn't say anything, Stephanie demanded, "Why did she order pizza then?"

I cleared my throat. "She thought you wanted it."

"I see." Stephanie said softly. She just stood there staring sadly at the inside of her refrigerator.

"Orange juice okay?" I asked as I started to rearrange things to reach the carton.

She just stood there quietly. Was she upset that we hadn't served her a regular banquet? But the pizza was her idea.

I got the juice and poured a glass, then shut the refrigerator. "Don't tell Mama that you know. Okay?" I asked. "Let her think I opened the refrigerator and got the drink for you."

"But we should talk about it," Stephanie said uneasily.

"You don't know my mother," I laughed sadly.

"Oh," she said. "I don't want to make any trouble."

As if Cinderella couldn't help but make problems for wicked stepsisters like me.

Before she left the kitchen, though, she paused at the doorway. It almost reminded me of a dancer getting focused so she could go on stage. When she sailed into the other room, she sounded as cheerful as before.

I wondered at the sudden change in her, but only a few minutes later she gave a polite yawn. "You'll have to excuse me. It's been a long day."

"Of course," Mama said. "Amy can show you where the towels and things are."

Stephanie got up and Jason, Andy, Mimi and Didi rushed to give her hugs.

While she was in the bathroom, I remembered to change the sheets on the lower bunk bed. I almost took my favorite pillow from my bed, but I thought of what Mama would say if she caught me so I took the lumpy one.

It was just as well because Mama stopped in to check on everything. "Good. Make her comfortable," she warned me.

I gave her a mock salute. "I'll try not to snore."

The joke was lost on Mama though. "Good girl," she said approvingly.

However, when I came back from my turn in the bathroom, I found Stephanie in the bunk bed instead.

"You're supposed to sleep on my bed," I protested.

Stephanie snuggled into her blanket as if it were a cocoon. "If you don't mind, I'd rather sleep here."

I slapped my hands against my sides in frustration. "It'd be worth my hide if Mama caught me in the bed. Please."

Reluctantly Stephanie unrolled herself from the blanket and sat up. She looked sad. "I don't want to get you in trouble either."

"Thanks," I sighed in relief.

"No, thank you," she said. Getting up, she crossed the room in her long-sleeved gown and zipped into the bed. "Good night."

She lay still as a statue under the covers.

I have a hard time sleeping in strange beds and it was even harder when I knew there was a stranger who had stolen both my family and my bed. I tried to remember Grandmother's pep talks because I figured it was going to be a long week.

Just as I was starting to drift off into sleep, though, I thought I heard an odd sound. It sounded like a sob. Could Stephanie be crying?

What did Cinderella have to be sad about? What had I . . . we done wrong?

I listened for more sobs, but there was only Stephanie's slow, regular breathing.

I figured that it had to be my imagination. As I felt sleep wrap itself around me like a warm cotton blanket, I was still wondering.

THIRTEEN

Home, Sweet Home

That Saturday morning, Robin and I drew some chuckles from Madame as we danced at the ball.

At the end of practice, Madame congratulated Robin and me. "Good, good little barnacles."

"Was that good or bad?" Robin whispered to me.

"Good. It means we're into our parts," I explained.

Robin still looked doubtful but she changed the subject. "So how's your guest working out?"

I thought of those strange moments last night when Stephanie had seemed so sad. "Okay, I guess, but I'll be glad when she's gone even if Didi and Mimi move back in."

Robin nodded sympathetically. "Even if a house guest is nice, it can still be hard sometimes. Did you have plans for today?"

I picked up my bag. "No. I thought I'd see what she wanted to do."

"Well, ask her if she wants to go down to Chinatown with Grandmother and me. Call us at Grand-mother's. We'll be there until one," Robin said, waving good-bye.

When I got home, I found Stephanie reading a magazine on the sofa. "Where're my brothers and sisters?"

"Mimi and Didi went over to a friend's house and Jason and Andy went out to a matinee with your mother," Stephanie smiled. "I didn't feel like seeing Wolf Warriors Twelve."

I had to laugh. "I wonder why? The comics are bad enough. I can't stand all that kicking and punching."

"They're not as bad as the Hong Kong comics." Stephanie swept the magazine in a large half-circle. "It's blood all over the page."

When she wasn't trying to impress my family, she seemed almost normal. "How long did you live in Hong Kong?" I asked.

"I was born there," Stephanie said, closing the magazine, "and Hong Kong has always been our home base. This is my first time living in the States."

"What nationality are you?" I asked.

"Well, my father is British but my mother was American." Stephanie set the magazine on a table. "So I'm a bit of a mongrel."

"So America is kind of like home," I said.

"Half of it anyway," Stephanie laughed nervously, "but I often feel like wherever I go, I'm like Moses—a stranger in a strange land."

I hadn't thought about Stephanie's viewpoint before. "Do things in America seem a little odd?"

"I used to watch television and read the magazines, but it's different than experiencing the real thing," Stephanie admitted. "I didn't meet my mother's relatives until this year."

I tried to think of what it would be like if I moved to Hong Kong after hearing mother's stories. It would be so strange for me that I'd be crying my head off all the time, not just in the evenings. "How did that go?"

Stephanie gave her head a little shake. "I'd rather not talk about it."

Whatever it was, I assume it hadn't been too good. Despite everything, I found myself warming to her. "Well, what would you like to do today? A friend's offered to take us into Chinatown."

"I'd love that," Stephanie said.

I made a quick call to Robin to tell her that we were coming. Then I took a shower and changed. Stephanie was sitting on the sofa with her purse on her lap, all ready to go.

I gave her points. She was trying to be a good guest. My conscience gave me a little pinch. "How'd you sleep last night?"

"Wonderful," she said with a chirpy smile. From the way she said that, I again thought I had been imagining hearing her cry.

On the way over to Robin's grandmother's, I told

Stephanie a little about her. "She's a real neat lady. She came from Hong Kong about a year ago. Now she's kind of become a group grandmother."

Stephanie looked interested. "Do you know what part of Hong Kong she lived in?"

"No, but you can ask her," I said. "One other thing, though—she uses canes because there's something wrong with her feet."

"Lily feet?" Stephanie asked curiously.

"What have lilies got to do with it?" I asked.

"It's a polite word for a woman with bound feet," Stephanie said. "In the bandages, the feet are supposed to be shaped like lilies."

"That's what she has, but how did you know?" I asked in amazement. "She won't tell anyone."

"I met several elderly ladies in Hong Kong who had that done to them when they were little girls," Stephanie said. "I wonder how she handles her feet?"

I misunderstood her question. "Well, she has the canes."

"No, I mean her secret," Stephanie asked.

"She keeps it pretty well," I said. "I just found out recently."

Stephanie gripped her stomach. "But when you keep it in inside, it just eats at you. How does she handle that?"

"I don't know, but she's very sensitive. Please don't say anything," I begged. "She might think I told you."

"I wouldn't dream of saying anything," Stephanie said, "if it would make her uncomfortable."

When Robin let us into her grandmother's apartment, she held a finger up to her lips. "Don't break their concentration."

The lights were off in the apartment so they could see the television screen better. "Got him!" Grandmother shouted as her wolf warrior pierced an enemy robot with a spear. She sat back satisfied as it exploded.

Next to her was a man about her age with thinning hair. "This darn joystick. My warrior never goes where I want it to," he said in exasperation.

Grandmother laughed. "If you're losing your coordination, maybe you shouldn't be driving."

"I'll show you," the man grunted and sent his wolf warrior scurrying after Grandmother.

"Robin, this is Miss—," I caught myself. "This is Stephanie."

"Glad to meet you," Robin whispered and shook Stephanie's hand.

She led us over to a sofa where we sat down and watched Grandmother and her friend laugh and play like two kids.

It only took a few minutes for her friend's wolf warrior to die a gruesome death. Closing his eyes, he threw back his head. "Not again," he moaned.

Grandmother punched a button to save the game

and teased, "You'd never make a wolf warrior. You're nothing but a pup."

He ran a hand through his thinning hair. "At least I'm still young."

"Grandmother," Robin said from the sofa, "this is Amy's guest, Stephanie."

Stephanie got to her feet quickly and bowed. "I'm so pleased to meet you," she said in flawless Chinese.

I stared at her because her Chinese was better than mine.

Grandmother turned around on the floor. "I'm pleased to meet you too," she said. "You speak Chinese excellently."

"I've lived in Hong Kong most of my life," Stephanie said.

Grandmother brightened. "Oh, where?"

They traded notes on Hong Kong for a while, remembering favorite places and winding up, as all Chinese conversations did, with places to eat.

"Speaking of eating," the man said, patting his stomach, "I'm starving."

Grandmother indicated the man. "This hungry man is my friend, Ah Wing."

"He's your boyfriend," Robin teased in English.

"He is not," Grandmother insisted, switching to English as well.

"I am too," Ah Wing laughed.

Whatever he was to Grandmother, they were certainly comfortable with one another. He got her canes for her and helped her to her feet.

There was an old taxi parked by the curb outside. Ah Wing strutted toward it like one of those fighter pilots in the war movies. Taking an old battered peaked cap from the dashboard, he set it on his head and adjusted it to a rakish angle. Then, stamping his feet on the ground like a soldier, he opened the doors for us. "Your carriage awaits."

With a wink, Robin shot into the back seat and pulled Stephanie with her. With a giggle, Stephanie grabbed my arm and yanked me in, too.

"No room, Grandmother," Robin laughed. "You'll have to sit up front with your boyfriend."

"He is not my boyfriend," Grandmother insisted. "I'm too old for such foolishness." However, she didn't look very upset to have to sit in front beside him.

On the way into Chinatown, Grandmother and Stephanie began to reminisce about movie theaters. As it turned out, they were both big fans of Jackie Chan movies.

"He's my all-time favorite," Stephanie said.

"Mine too," Grandmother beamed.

To my surprise, he was also Robin's favorite.

Like a good hostess, Grandmother noticed how quiet I was and tried to draw me into a conversation. "Do you like Jackie Chan movies, Amy?"

"No," I said. "I don't like the violence."

"As a rule, neither do I," Stephanie said, "but I enjoy the humor."

"Do you remember the time when he fought wearing skirts?" Robin asked excitedly.

That set off a new round of reminiscing and laughter. I felt as if Stephanie was even trying to steal my friends.

The streets in Chinatown were jammed with traffic so it took us a while to get to our destination—a beat-up old restaurant called the Celestial Forest. Ah Wing double-parked his cab to let us out before he went hunting for parking. When the cars started to honk their horns, he stuck his head out of his window and shouted. "Just hold your horses," he said, adding a few oaths in Chinese.

Stephanie got out with a broad grin and then just stood there looking around. "This is just like home."

Inside, the customers greeted Grandmother and Robin, and a waiter in a red jacket and bow tie came over. "You're late," he said with a frown.

"I was playing a video game," Grandmother said, pantomiming moving a joystick.

"We brought guests," Grandmother said, introducing us to the waiter.

The restaurant was a lively place. A lot of the customers must have come here regularly because they seemed to know one another. They held conversations by shouting across the room, Grandmother included.

Every now and then she tossed down a cup of hot tea to keep her vocal cords limber. Robin joined in too when she could get a word in edgewise.

Ah Wing strolled in by the time the soup came in. His cap was off, so I assumed he was off duty. The greetings to Ah Wing were a little rougher—more like when Jason and his friends got together to play. In fact, most of the regular customers seemed to be men.

A man in a red windbreaker turned around. "You know what this is, little girl?" he asked Stephanie.

Stephanie's face lit up when she saw what the soup was. "Shark's fin. Yum."

He seemed surprised that she would like it. "You don't mind eating it?"

"I love it," she said.

He got a sly look. "Say, you know what they call the fishermen who catch sharks?"

Stephanie replied in Chinese, "I believe they call them Lefty. That's a very old joke."

Ah Wing roared, "She's grabbed all your tens, Ah Bock."

"Strong eyes and weak eyes," Stephanie said, also in Chinese.

I turned to Robin and whispered, "What'd she say?"

Robin could only shake her head. "I don't know."

Ah Bock sat back. "How did a girl like you learn about dominoes?"

"I've won my share from the boxes," Stephanie explained.

Ah Wing nudged Ah Bock. "She speaks Chinese better than your grandkids."

Ah Bock scratched his head. "Aw, you coached her on what to say."

"He tells the same shark joke to all newcomers," Grandmother explained to Stephanie and me, then turned to Ah Bock. "She was born in Hong Kong."

"You went to the gambling places?" Ah Bock asked.

"No, the maids taught me," Stephanie said.

"What's the box?" I asked her.

"At the start of the game, everyone puts a stake into the box," Stephanie explained. "A popular game is called 'grasping many tens' and weak eyes and strong eyes refer to parts of that game."

I felt as lost as much as Stephanie seemed to feel on home ground. In no time, the regulars were teasing her and she was teasing back.

The lunch itself was tasty, but Grandmother was the first to sample each dish and critique it to the waiter who would relay it to the kitchen.

The last dish was a pressed duck in a coating of taro which the cook himself brought out. "I tried to follow your recipe as close as I could," he said anxiously to Grandmother.

Grandmother sampled a piece. "You got the sauce right, Ng. But next time leave it in longer."

"I'll get it right the next time," Ng said. "Thanks so much for giving me the recipes."

"I didn't know you had been a chef," I said to her.

Grandmother turned the lazy susan on the table so that the dish was in front of Stephanie. "I'm not, but I like to eat, and over the years you collect recipes."

"Well, it's all been wonderful," Stephanie said. She used her chopsticks easily—as if they were an extra set of fingers.

When we were done, Stephanie tried to pick up the lunch check, but Grandmother wrestled her for it. In an American restaurant, the scene might have drawn a lot of stares, but here there was a lot a of good-natured joking. Ah Bock even placed a bet with Ah Wing that Stephanie would win.

However, age and experience finally won over youth and reflexes. "Your money's no good here," Grandmother announced as she waved the check triumphantly in the air.

"But how can I ever eat with you again," Stephanie said, trying one last desperate snatch.

Grandmother pinched Stephanie's arm. "Be a good girl, dear," she scolded.

It was only then that Stephanie settled back. I knew the art of pinching pretty well from having dealt with the brats. That had been a grade-A pinch if I'd ever seen one, but Stephanie was actually smiling.

"All right, Grandmother," she said.

I glanced at Robin to see if it bothered her to have Stephanie adopt her grandmother too, but Robin was grinning. I guess she was used to sharing her grandmother since all her friends had adopted her grandmother for their own.

After lunch, we went shopping with Grandmother. Stephanie pointed at clusters of little orange fruits about the size of large marbles. "Those loquat look good," she said to me. "Does your mother like them?"

"She loves them," I said.

I couldn't have told a bad loquat from a good one, but Stephanie was as fussy as Grandmother when it came to picking fruit. When she finally found a cluster she liked, Grandmother nodded approvingly.

"Good choice," she said.

Then, when Stephanie went to the cash register, she said in Chinese, "These have bruises, you know. You really shouldn't be selling them."

The clerk seemed surprised to hear her talking Chinese, but shrugged. "Then put them back."

"Stephanie," I said, embarrassed.

Stephanie was obviously enjoying herself. "I did this all the time in Hong Kong," Stephanie said.

I'd never heard of anyone bargaining over vegetables in Chinatown, but Stephanie did until she got ten cents knocked off.

Grandmother and Ah Wing were smiling at her performance. "You make a better Chinese than me," Ah Wing said.

"In Hong Kong, they expect to bargain," Stephanie said.

From the sullen looks of the clerk, I don't think they did in San Francisco.

"Next time you do the shopping," Grandmother laughed.

Stephanie clutched her purchases against her stomach. "I haven't had this much fun in a long time."

"So you grew up in Hong Kong?" Robin asked.

"Yes, it was our home base until last year," Stephanie said, adjusting her grip.

"You didn't even come home to the States for holidays?" Robin wondered.

Stephanie shook her head. "Home was Hong Kong."

"Do you ever miss it?" Grandmother asked.

Some hostess I was. I'd never thought of the most obvious question.

I saw a spark of recognition in Stephanie's eyes. "You too?" she asked.

"Often," Grandmother sighed.

As they chatted in Chinese about what they missed about Hong Kong, I tailed them down the street.

"Where is the best tea shop in Chinatown?" Stephanie asked. "I'd like something special."

"I know just the place," Grandmother said, and led us to a shop with drawers that went up either side.

A clerk in a blouse with a big bow smiled and called a greeting in Chinese to Grandmother.

"What were you looking for?" Grandmother asked Stephanie.

"I'd like 'dragon tear'," Stephanie said in Chinese.

If the clerk was surprised to hear Stephanie speak Chinese, she didn't show it. "That is very expensive."

"Yes, I know," Stephanie said, opening her purse.

"Are you sure, dear?" Grandmother asked.

"I heard Mrs. Chin say she loved it," Stephanie said.

That was the first I'd ever heard that. I couldn't help thinking that Stephanie not only made a better daughter and sister than me, but she was even a better Chinese.

In fact, I was beginning to think she could live my life better than me. I wondered if the stepsisters felt this dazed as they watched Cinderella whirl around the ballroom floor as the belle of the ball.

FOURTEEN

Princess Perfect

Mama, of course, loved the loquat, and she adored the tea. "We'll save it for a special occasion," she said, putting it in a tin.

"But I bought it for you to use," Stephanie said.

"And I will," she said.

The loquat, though, were fair game. By Sunday morning she was already finishing the last of them as I practiced some of the dances in the living room. Stephanie played DJ, advancing my new CD to the tracks I needed.

When I was done, she even clapped. "You're as good as the Zlyuka we saw at the San Francisco Ballet."

I thought she was laying it on a little thick, but I said, "Thank you."

"So what are you girls going to do today?" Mama asked as she peeled the last loquat.

Stephanie looked up from the pink arts section of the paper. "Today I have a lunch with some acquaintances."

Great, I thought, today I get a break from playing the hostess, but then Stephanie turned to me. "Would you like to come with me, Amy? Lou-Lou's a ballerina too."

"She won't be expecting me," I said.

"Lou-Lou told me I could bring a guest," Stephanie said. "It'll be lots of fun."

As much fun as jumping off the Golden Gate Bridge. The last thing I wanted was an afternoon with Stephanie's ritzy friends. "I really have a lot of stuff to do."

Andy, though, was eager to go wherever there was free food. "I'll go."

Stephanie smiled indulgently at him. "It's just for girls our age, Andy. We'll do something else together."

"Like the new Wolf Warriors movie?" Andy asked.

"You've already seen that with Mama," I said.

"It's a classic," Andy argued.

Stephanie had more patience than I did. Despite what she had said before, she nodded. "Sure."

Andy never knew when to quit. "With popcorn?"

"With popcorn," Stephanie promised.

Mimi yanked at her sleeve. "What about me?" Jason and Didi were also getting ready to ask.

"The rest of you too," Stephanie laughed. "Maybe we can all go together after the lunch."

The loquat formed a lump in Mama's cheek as she chewed the flesh from the large seed. "Go with Stephanie to the lunch," she said to me. "Your chores can wait."

"Please say yes," Stephanie said.

I couldn't understand why she wanted me to go. "Shouldn't you call your hostess at least and see if it's okay?"

"Don't give it another thought," Stephanie said.

Mama took the large loquat seed from her mouth. "Then it's settled," she said, giving me a firm look.

Well, I thought to myself, *maybe I am as wrong about her friends as I had been about Stephanie.* I reminded myself of what Madame had said. Change was good. I had to be open to the world.

I might never become a real Cinderella like Stephanie, but at least I could try.

So I got dressed in some of Stephanie's gifts, deciding that Mama's home-made clothes might draw stares.

As we walked to the bus stop, Stephanie sighed. "I wish Father had leased a flat here."

I couldn't see why anyone would trade her palace for our ordinary little flats. "Why?"

"It reminds me a little of Hong Kong—only not so crowded," Stephanie said. "Hong Kong's the only place I feel at home."

"I wish I could see all the cities and stuff you have," I confessed.

Stephanie smiled sadly. "Sometimes I think it would mean as much if I had seen them on postcards."

She sounded so lonely at that moment that I stared at her.

"Most people would give their right hand to travel to all the places you have," I said, trying to make her feel better.

"It doesn't mean much if you don't have someone to share it with," Stephanie said. "It must be so nice to have real roots. You have your family, your friends and your schools."

If I didn't know it was crazy, I would have said she sounded like she envied me. She almost made it sound like she was the stepsister and I was Cinderella.

There weren't as many buses on Sunday so it took a while to get over to Pacific Heights.

The houses were even bigger and fancier than on Stephanie's street. I had been calling Stephanie's place a palace, but these buildings really were.

We stopped by the biggest. It reminded me of a white and pink wedding cake. It sat behind a large iron fence painted black, and the spikes on top were coated in a gold color.

Stephanie punched a button and spoke into the intercom. "Lou-Lou?"

There wasn't any reply, but we heard a buzz at the gate. When I shoved at it, it swung in on its well-oiled hinges.

As we began to walk up the brick path, I couldn't

help giggling. "I feel just like Dorothy visiting the Wizard of Oz."

Stephanie chuckled. "When you meet Lou-Lou, you'll see how true that is. She puts on a flashy show, but underneath it all, she's just a humbug." It was the first unkind words I'd heard from Stephanie, and I hadn't expected them to be about her rich friends. So I just stared, but Stephanie headed straight for the door and rang the doorbell.

Inside, I heard rapid footsteps and then a woman in a gray-and-white maid's outfit opened the door. "Stephanie Sinclair and Amy Chin to see Lou-Lou," Stephanie said.

"This way," the maid said.

I could have found Lou-Lou by following the loud music blasting from the stereo. The volume was so high that the half-dozen girls had to shout at one another. They seemed to be having a good time, shrieking over some joke.

They all had willowy builds on which their expensive clothes fit very well.

"Miss Stephanie and a guest," the maid said from the doorway.

"Stephie," Lou-Lou said, turning with a smile. She had her hair pulled back like a ballerina, and the straight posture of a dancer. She lost it when she saw me.

"This is my hostess, Amy Chin," Stephanie said, indicating me.

The other girls fell silent while Lou-Lou eyed me from head to toe.

I was ready to bolt for the door, but Stephanie slipped her arm through mine in an unbreakable hold. "You said I could bring a guest."

"I'm delighted Amy could come too," Lou-Lou said, but her expression said: What are you doing crashing my lunch?

"Thank you," I said, wishing I could melt into the woodwork.

"Amy is studying the ballet too," Stephanie said.

Lou-Lou suddenly looked interested. "Oh, really. Where?"

I named Madame's school.

Lou-Lou pressed a fingertip against her chin. "I'm afraid I haven't heard of that one. Where is it?"

Proudly, I gave the address.

Lou-Lou drew her eyebrows together as she smiled. "Oh, it's one of those cute little neighborhood schools."

"It's a very good school," I bristled.

Stephanie tried to change the topic as she sat down. "Where do you study ballet, Lou-Lou?"

Lou-Lou's school was a prestigious one. Many of its students moved into the official school of the San Francisco Ballet.

"I'm understudying the role of Giselle," she said.

That was a famous ballet and far more ambitious

than our school's recital, but Stephanie didn't realize that. "Amy's studying for a recital too."

"Oh, what role?" Lou-Lou asked.

I perched uneasily on the edge of the sofa cushion. "A stepsister in *Cinderella*."

"Ah . . . how . . . challenging," Lou-Lou said.

She didn't have a clue about the demands of the role. I had effectively killed any conversation for several minutes and we just stared at one another.

Finally Lou-Lou rose. "Well, we're all here. I'll see what's holding up lunch." She left the room as if grateful to escape.

A blonde girl turned to Stephanie. "We were just talking about our favorite places to ski. Where do you like to go, Stephanie? Aspen?"

It was strange to see Stephanie squirm uncomfortably. "I don't ski, Cynthia," she said.

Cynthia laughed as if it were a quaint notion. "Who actually skis? I mean, where do you go to party?"

Another girl joined her. "Remember that time you spilled tea on your outfit and ruined it?"

Cynthia began to giggle. "I went around pretending I'd gotten snow on it."

"You must have a favorite place, Stephie," the other girl said.

Stephanie bit her lip. "Actually, I've never seen snow," she admitted, and tried to draw me into the conversation. "Where do you like to go, Amy?"

"I've never been skiing," I confessed.

Everybody fell silent at that, simply looking away in embarrassment while the music blared from the stereo.

Fortunately Lou-Lou reappeared in the doorway. "Lunch is served, ladies."

I just couldn't take it anymore. Lou-Lou and the others were even worse than I had expected Stephanie to be.

I slapped a hand against my stomach. "I'm sorry. I haven't been feeling well. I really shouldn't have come."

Lou-Lou looked relieved, but said, "Oh, what a shame."

Stephanie got up. "I'd better help you home."

"No, you stay with your friends," I said, wanting only to escape as fast as I could.

Stephanie clamped her hand on my arm in an iron grip again. "I wouldn't think of leaving you alone at a time like this."

"I'll have the maid call a cab," Lou-Lou said, and started to turn.

That would mean waiting. "No, what I need the most is to walk," I said.

"Yes, the fresh air would do you good," Stephanie chimed in.

We left as quickly as politeness allowed. As the gate shut behind us, I got ready to apologize to Stephanie, but she breathed a deep sigh of relief. "Thank heaven we got away. I don't know why I ever let my father talk me into going. I really owe you."

FIFTEEN

The Stranger

I stopped dead in my tracks. "What do you mean?"

She gave an apologetic shrug. "I couldn't have gone without your support. It was a mean trick to make you come with me. Do you hate me now?"

I glanced back at the cake palace. "I thought they were your friends."

Stephanie laughed harshly. "Hardly. Lou-Lou's just the daughter of a woman my father works with. I went through that little charade just to please my father. He was so insistent that I go, but this morning I starting losing my nerve."

I was actually starting to feel sorry for Stephanie.

She stepped over a crack in the sidewalk. "He was worried that I didn't know anyone my age here."

Or class, I thought. "You'd meet kids if you went to school," I said.

Stephanie gave a little skip so she could avoid the

next crack. "The schools are full of students like Lou-Lou."

So Cinderella didn't lead such a charmed life after all. I had never thought about the other side of the palace and expensive clothes. If Mama's amah job could be hard on me, I guess the princess lifestyle could be hard on Stephanie. "But everyone who meets you loves you," I blurted out.

How could someone with her sweet temperament and all her talents not make friends?

She studied the pavement. "I make people nervous."

She said something in another dialect of Chinese.

"I only speak Cantonese," I said.

"It's a line from a very old poem," Stephanie explained. " 'I am just the flower petal drifting alone in the winter wind.' "

The only sad poems I knew were from rock songs. And none of them were that sad or that lonely or cold. She made me feel like shivering. "But you're not alone. My little brothers and sisters would trade me for you any day. And I think Mama would make the swap even faster."

Stephanie whirled around to stare at me. "But what about you? What if you could swap me right now for . . . let's say, Mimi?"

I could feel myself blushing so I looked away.

"You see?" said Stephanie. "I try and try to make friends, but it never works in the end."

I thought about some of the mysteries. "The comic books were new ones you bought just to give away, weren't they?"

Stephanie started to walk away. "Since we just got here from Hong Kong, I don't have much to discard."

I had to hurry to catch her. "And the clothes?" I asked.

"No, those were old ones." She wrapped her arms around herself as if she were suddenly cold. "I . . . just didn't need them anymore."

We walked along for a half-block before I tried to encourage her. "There's a lot to like about you. You don't have to give a lot of presents."

She seemed uneasy. "But people like presents even if they don't like me."

"That's not true," I tried to reassure her.

"But . . ." Stephanie hesitated.

"But what?" I asked.

"Why don't you like me?" she asked in a small voice.

My first reaction was to lie, but Stephanie was smart enough to see right through it. So instead I thought about it as we walked along. Finally I took a deep breath and let it out. "It's just you're so . . . perfect."

Stephanie began her game of stepping over the cracks again. "I'm far from that."

I gave a skip so I could keep pace. "You can't do anything wrong in my mother's eyes," I said. It was a stepsister-ish thing to say, and I instantly regretted it.

"And I can't do anything right in my father's," Stephanie said crisply, almost biting out the words.

I had to scratch my head over that one. "I can't think of anyone having standards that high. What does he want?"

"I have to be the best at everything—the best student, the best athlete, the best daughter." She gave a little puff as she landed hard after a hop. "I also have be the best hostess at dinners."

I stopped in surprise. "You mean adult dinners?"

She looked over her shoulder. "Yes, he expects me to take my mother's place."

It was bad enough he was asking her to be the perfect child, but she was awfully young to be a perfect adult too. I had resented the way my mother had asked me to take her place so often. In some ways, though, Stephanie'd had to mature even faster.

"My mother makes your father sound like he's perfect too," I said.

Stephanie chuckled. "He's perfect at doing his job. That's his only concern."

"But he's always kind to my mother," I said.

Stephanie seemed startled. "Is that what she says?" She shrugged. "Maybe she doesn't want to worry you."

I felt bad for resenting my mother's trips to the palace. Maybe it wasn't such a dream job after all. Perhaps she had been trying to protect me by only telling me the positive things about the job.

"Sometimes I feel so . . ." Stephanie heaved her shoulders up and down. "So trapped."

I remembered how I had felt those first few days when Mama had been working for the Sinclairs. "Like you're in a cage," I said.

Stephanie's eyes lit in recognition. "Only the cage is invisible so no one else can see it. You're the only one who knows it's there."

So at least we had that in common. I found myself liking Stephanie again. "Do you really want to make people feel more comfortable around you?"

"Absolutely," she said.

"Remember what Madame said about Cinderella?" I asked.

She nodded. "It's about re-making yourself."

"So re-make yourself into a slob like the rest of us," I said.

"What?" Stephanie laughed nervously.

"I'll give you lessons," I grinned.

"What will Father say?" Stephanie asked, worried.

"If he's your father, he'll want you to be happy," I argued, "and you'll only be happy if you have friends."

"I suppose so," she said uncertainly.

I backed up my argument with the ultimate authority—Madame—though I changed the wording a little on the stepsister principle. "Look. There's two kinds of people: those who can change and those who don't. The people who do change can maybe become happy.

The people who don't stay miserable. Now which do you want to be?"

Stephanie didn't say anything until we reached the bus stop. "I want to be like you."

"Me?" I snorted. "What for? I'm the worst example."

"Because even if you don't like a person, you're willing to listen to her," Stephanie said. "So thank you."

"I like you," I said, and added truthfully, "sort of."

Stephanie put up a hand. "So I'll try to change."

The changes started right when we got home. The brats pounced on us as soon as we came through the door as if they had been waiting all this time.

Later, when Stephanie treated us all to the movie, the kids dragged her over to the refreshment stand. "How about some popcorn?" Jason asked, pointing at a bucket bigger than his head.

"And candy," Didi said, pointing at a big box of mints.

"No, no, that one," Andy said, pointing to another box.

Stephanie started to reach for her purse. "And what else?"

I cleared my throat. "Remember your promise," I said.

She was torn between her promise to me and my brothers' and sisters' eager faces. "We don't want to spoil dinner though, do we?" she asked.

Much to their shock, Stephanie wound up buying the smallest container of popcorn.

Naturally, the kids began quarreling over it five minutes into the movie. "Don't hog it, Jason," Mimi complained.

Stephanie started to get up. "Maybe I should get another."

I grabbed her arm. "Slobs-ville," I reminded her. "Let them settle it among themselves."

She slumped back down. "But—"

"Hey, it takes work being imperfect," I said, glancing at the brats. Mimi was squinting at the floor rather than the movie screen. I just hoped she wasn't looking for stray popcorn.

And that evening, much to Jason's disappointment, Stephanie did not buy pizzas. Instead, we cooked the food Mama had prepared.

"You be our guest, Mrs. Chin," Stephanie told her.

Mama was uncomfortable, though, having Stephanie cook for her. "Don't you want some help?"

"No, we'll just use what's in the fridge," I said.

"And I'd like to learn my way around a kitchen," Stephanie said.

So I got out our old wok. Years of cooking had depositing a black coating on the rounded insides. Along the rim, though, the black gave way to an iridescent sheen.

Stephanie ran a finger along the rainbow band. "How pretty. It reminds me of the insides of an abalone shell."

Everything about our little kitchen fascinated her. "You haven't spent much time in kitchens, have you?" I asked.

"It's all I can do to make a peanut butter-and-jelly sandwich," she confessed.

"So there's something you're not perfect at," I said.

"Guilty," she admitted.

"I can't wait till you pick it up though. Then you can be the cook and I can be the supervisor," I teased. "First, we'll start on the rice."

Mama didn't believe in rice cookers or in that awful American instant rice. I'd had it once at Leah's and it had tasted like mush.

"First, we have to wash the rice." I put several cupfuls of rice into the pot.

"Shouldn't you measure?" Stephanie asked.

"By now, I can judge by eye and weight," I said and adjusted the tap so that the water was lukewarm. Then I filled the pot and began to swirl the rice around so that the water turned milky. "My home-ec teacher says you wash away the nutrients, but the rice doesn't stick this way. And every now and then there's stuff in the rice you have to take out."

A couple little bits of chaff floated on the top like little bugs, and I chased them with my fingertips until I trapped them one by one and threw them away.

I set the lid on the pot, leaving only a crack so I could pour the water out. "Now you do it," I said.

Stephanie, though, used too much water. Grains of rice went flying out of the pot and into the sink under the jet of hot water. "Sorry," she laughed.

"We all make mistakes." I winked, then added a little more rice to make up for what we had lost.

This time Stephanie adjusted the flow so it was hardly more than a trickle. Then she swirled her hand around inside the pot. "It's very restful, isn't it?"

I thought of all the other kitchen chores. "I've got a lot more restful things ahead for you."

We let the rice come to a boil. Then I turned the flame down to simmer and swirled the rice around one more time before I set the lid down. Next to me, I could see Stephanie's lips moving as if she were memorizing the steps.

Once that was done, I put some oil into the wok and when it was sizzling, I put in some pieces of cut-up chicken.

Mama had a pair of wooden cooking chopsticks that were twice as long and thick as the regular ones. I cooked the first batch and then turned to Stephanie.

"Have you ever used these before?" I asked.

"No, but I think I can get the hang of it," she said. She proved to be a quick student.

I slapped her on the back. "Congratulations. From the way you can handle those chopsticks, you're being promoted to chief of bacon tomorrow morning."

She looked up from the chicken sizzling in the oil. "I

don't know a lot about cooking, but don't you use a spatula?"

"Not in this kitchen," I said. "It's a lot easier to turn over bacon with chopsticks. Also for getting reluctant muffins out of the toaster."

"What won't they think of next," Stephanie said, giving her head a shake. She was sweaty and there were oil stains on her apron and somehow a bit of flour had striped her cheek. However, I don't think I had ever seen her happier.

"I think now would be a nice time to have that special tea you bought," I said.

"You're absolutely right. Where's that lovely teapot?" Stephanie asked.

I hesitated, wondering if we should risk the fragile teapot. And yet I hesitated to disappoint Stephanie. "Well . . ."

However, Stephanie was already searching the cabinets. "It must be here somewhere."

"Maybe I should ask Mama first," I said.

Stephanie had knelt and was rummaging around in the lower cabinets. "Why? We used it with the pizzas the other night."

That was true. And we had used it for Auntie Ruby's tea. And this was an occasion just as special. How often did we celebrate Stephanie's finding a family? I was feeling so good that I didn't stop to think. "It's right here."

Kneeling, I got out the antique teapot.

"It's so lovely," Stephanie said, admiring it. "I could look at it all day."

Carefully I set the teapot on the table and gave it a quick wipe with a towel and then stepped back. It was our one possession that we could match against the Sinclairs' things. "It's been in the family for generations."

Stephanie turned it around gently with a fingertip. "It's a real treasure."

I gave Stephanie a playful shove back toward the stove. "Hey, back to work," I said as I got out the tea that Stephanie had bought. "Or I'm going to have to bust you down to dishwasher."

Stephanie snapped off a salute with her free hand. "Yes, ma'am," she said and resumed her station.

I filled the kettle with water and set it on the burner. Then I began to cook beside her.

When the water had boiled, I got out the tea ball. When I opened the bag, the fragrant aroma smelled heavenly. I couldn't wait to try it as I packed it into a tea ball and then dumped it into the pot.

Stephanie was only trying to be helpful. "Here's the water."

I didn't stop to think, or I might have remembered the other part of Mama's ritual sooner. As it was, I only recalled the next step just as Stephanie started to pour the hot water directly into the teapot.

"Wait. I think we have to warm the pot first," I said.

"What?" Stephanie looked at me but her wrist continued to twist so that a silvery stream of water flooded the teapot. When it was about halfway full, the fragile walls just seemed to explode. Pieces went sailing like parts of a bomb. I saw the dragon fly before my eyes.

Mama's precious teapot had shattered, and my world with it.

SIXTEEN

Trouble

The boiling water splashed on my apron. "Ow," I said jumping back.

Stephanie had gotten the worst of it. The kettle dropped from her hand, splashing more hot water on her. "Oh."

She gave a backward hop, slamming against the sink.

"Are you all right?" I asked.

Stephanie was bent double over the sink. She jerked back a wet sleeve. "I'm fine."

To my horror I saw an ugly red line across her wrist. "You're burned."

"Leave me alone!" Stephanie began to cry as she leaned over the sink.

I desperately wanted to be helpful. "We should get you to the emergency room."

Stephanie twisted her head and snapped, "I'm fine."

I'd been to the emergency room once when Jason

had suddenly gotten sick. It hadn't been fun. "If you don't want to go to the emergency room, my friend Leah's mother is a doctor."

She glared at me. "If I tell you that I'm fine, then I am."

"But your wrist—" I started to protest.

"It's just something I already had," she said, jerking her sleeve back down. "I want you to forget all about it."

"It looked pretty bad. How did you get it?" I asked.

The words slipped out of her softly like air leaking from a balloon. "None of your business."

As Stephanie started to kneel to pick up the pieces, I offered, "Let me do that."

Stephanie didn't say anything. Bending over, she delicately fished up the little dragon and another piece. Grimly she tried to fit them together.

"Maybe we could glue the pieces together," I suggested.

Stephanie clutched the little dragon to her and she screwed her eyes shut as if in pain. Suddenly her shoulders began to shake and tears flowed down her cheeks. She shuddered as she expelled her breath in a large sob.

I don't think Mama would have been as upset about the teapot. I went over to Stephanie, hearing bits of the antique teapot crunch under my feet. For a moment, I felt like I was walking over Stephanie's broken heart and not the teapot.

Mimi came in with an empty glass. "What's wrong? Are you all right, Stephanie?"

"We had an accident," she said, rocking back and forth.

Mimi put a hand to her mouth when she saw the broken teapot. "Did Mama say you could use it?" she asked.

"Well, I . . ." I paused. I didn't want to say Stephanie had done it. After all, she was just starting to feel at home with us. Swallowing, I muttered, "No, it's my fault. But we used it for the pizza and for that tea with Auntie Ruby."

Mimi took a step backwards as if she wanted to distance herself from the disaster. "You should have asked," Mimi said.

That's what I had wanted to do, but Stephanie had been so insistent. I knew I couldn't say that. I had to take the blame. "I'll make it up to her somehow."

"It was an antique," Mimi said. "If you worked a million-billion years, you couldn't replace it."

"Mimi, you're missing the best part," Jason said, and then stopped and looked in the doorway. "I'm glad it wasn't me."

"You're going to be grounded for life." Mimi backed up another step and bumped against Jason.

Jason was so shocked that for once he didn't shove her away. "For sure, Mama's going to cut out your ballet lessons."

"I'll get a job," I said frantically. "Lots of them."

Stephanie wiped her tears away abruptly. "But it was my fault."

"It was my fault. I should have stopped you," I said.

Stephanie finished drying her face. "But you were afraid to say no to me. Everyone is. Everyone acts like I am made out of glass."

How do you explain the Cinderella effect to Cinderella herself? "People think of you as special," I said.

Stephanie turned on her knees, tossing the dishtowel back onto the dish rack. "Oh, I'm special all right." She rose slowly. "Would your mother really make you give up ballet?"

"She'll be mad, but she'll get over it," I said. At least, I hoped that was the truth.

"But we can't let that happen even for a little while. I know how much you love ballet," Stephanie said. She straightened. "I'm not going to let you get hurt because of me."

Stephanie looked thoughtful. "I have an idea," she said slowly. "I'll get the one from home."

"But that was your mother's," I said.

"It was going to be mine anyway," Stephanie said, and squeezed my arm. "Don't worry. I won't let anything happen to you." Maybe there was a reason that Cinderella really had an effect on people. Maybe if I wanted to have that effect, I had to think more of other people and less about myself.

"I can't ask that of you," I said. "I'll take my medicine from Mama."

Stephanie shook her head. "But it's not your fault.

It's all mine. I insisted on using the teapot, and I was the one who broke it." At that moment, the timer dinged. "The rice," Stephanie said, whirling.

I smelled something burning. "Oh, no. The chicken."

The oil had all burned up in the wok, which was starting to send out smoke.

"Is everything all right?" Mama called from the living room. "Where is everyone?"

Stephanie took charge. "Mimi, get your water. Jason, get back in there. And if you ever want another comic book from me, don't say a word to Mama. Nothing's wrong. Got it?"

Jason looked stunned. He was used to threats from me, but not from Stephanie.

"Got it," he said meekly, and left.

Mimi skirted the wet wreckage and got her glass of water and then went back to the living room.

"I'll clean up," Stephanie said, turning to get the broom and dust pan. "Amy, you try to salvage the chicken."

I snapped off the gas burner under the rice and asked, "Is that scar the reason why you wear long sleeves all the time?" I ran through the gifts of her clothes she had given me. Everything had short sleeves.

Stephanie began to sweep the damp debris into a pile. "Yes," she admitted reluctantly. "But don't tell anyone."

"But there's nothing to be ashamed of," I said. "Plenty of people have accidents that leave marks. And can't you get an operation to cover up the scar?"

Stephanie picked some wet pieces from the dust pan and threw them into the trash can so hard that they broke into even smaller bits. "Just drop it. Okay? I feel about the scar like Robin's grandmother feels about her feet."

"Okay," I said, more mystified than ever.

Dinner was a tense affair. We had to smile and act as if nothing had happened. But we nearly lost it when Mama started to go for the special teapot.

"No, I'd rather have soda," I said.

"You can't hurt Miss Stephanie's feelings," Mama frowned.

"I'd prefer soda too," Stephanie said hastily.

"Me three," Mimi said.

"Ow," Jason said when I kicked him under the table. "Yeah, soda," he said. He turned and glared at Andy and Didi. "They want sodas too."

Mama shrugged. "Well, it's really not worth heating up a pot of tea for just me. I guess I'll just have water."

After dinner both Stephanie and I went to bed early. Even Jason and Mimi got the other two to give up their usual marathon of cartoons.

Stephanie got ready for bed first so by the time I finished, Stephanie lay huddled on the bed, rolled up in the blanket.

"Stephanie?" I whispered.

Stephanie didn't say anything so I slipped under the covers. However, sleep didn't come quickly. As I lay there, I remembered when Stephanie had guessed Grandmother's secret. What had she said? Something about a secret eating at your insides.

What was she so ashamed of? Whatever it was, I was going to do my best to protect Stephanie as much as she wanted to protect me.

SEVENTEEN

What's His Is His

The next afternoon, I can't say that my mind was on ballet. Robin was as good as ever. She combined Eveline's grace with Thomas' comedy. I'm afraid I just walked through my part. Normally whenever Eveline danced, I watched her because it was such a treat. I avoided Madame when I left.

It was late in the afternoon when I got home. Stephanie called me into the bedroom as soon as she heard me.

My brothers and sisters were already waiting. Andy was hopping up and down with impatience. "I know a secret, a secret."

"And don't you tell," Stephanie said, and wagged a finger at him.

"We've been waiting for you all afternoon," Mimi complained.

Stephanie led me over to a shopping bag where

there was a fuzzy ball inside. "I think this is an exact match."

Lifting out the ball, she unwrapped several protective layers of sweaters. The final sweater was dusty—I suppose from the teapot. It was the exact same dragon teapot.

"It even has the same marks," Mimi said.

"See?" Carefully Stephanie lifted it up to show me the bottom. The marks were the same.

Relief flooded over me. I couldn't figure out how Stephanie came up with such a huge miracle.

"Are you sure?" I asked.

"It's going to be mine someday so I can do what I like," Stephanie said, setting it back into the bag. "I couldn't sneak home until I finished my lessons here and my history tutor made me go over the Constitution."

"Are you sure it's okay?" I asked.

"My father hardly knows when I'm gone. How's he going to notice an old teapot?" She picked up the shopping bag. "Now we just have to smuggle this into the kitchen."

I motioned her to wait, peeking into the hallway. No sign of Mama. So far so good. I motioned to the kids. "You go ahead and run interference."

Andy grinned. "Oh, boy. This is just like one of the Wolf Warrior adventures."

The four of them began to tiptoe down the hallway.

"Don't be so obvious," I sighed.

"Right," Mimi said, starting to shuffle instead.

"I think they can write off careers as spies," I whispered to Stephanie. I nodded for her to go ahead while I guarded her back. "I thought your father spent a lot of time with you," I said in a low voice. "What about all the season subscriptions you have?"

Stephanie shrugged. "He uses them as gifts for his business associates. He only needs me as his official hostess." I think she was enjoying sharing a secret with me. "If it isn't a lot of his boring business acquaintances, then it's their children."

"Like Lou-Lou," I shuddered.

"She actually wasn't as bad as some of them," Stephanie said.

No wonder she had longed for a normal family—not that I thought of ourselves as a model one. Maybe we'd gotten off to a rocky start, but I was going to do my best to make her feel like she had one with us.

At that moment, though, I heard a door open. It was Mama coming out of her bedroom.

"There you are, Amy," she said.

"Go on," I whispered to Stephanie.

However, as Stephanie tried to continue, Mama called to her. "Wait, Stephanie. I just heard from your father."

Stephanie halted and turned, trying to keep the shopping bag behind her. "Oh, how is he?"

Mama was smiling. "He called from the airplane. He finished his business early so he came back. He's going to swing by and pick you up."

"I thought I had a whole week here," Stephanie said, disappointed.

"I'm sure he misses you," Mama said.

"My father never has a spare moment. It's always business," Stephanie said, staring back down the hallway.

"Well, I'm flattered you want to put up with my monsters for a longer period of time," Mama said. "When he comes by, you can ask him if you can stay the rest of the week."

As Mama passed, I caught her shoulder. "Mama, can I ask you something?"

Mama stopped. "On what?"

I jerked my head for Stephanie to go on. Of course, that meant I had to come up with something. "Mama, what's Mr. Sinclair really like?"

"He's a very nice man," she said. Mama's face was a smiling mask. She ought to learn how to play poker.

"I've been talking to Stephanie," I said, lowering my voice. "She says he can be tough sometimes."

Mama was uncomfortable criticizing an employer. "He's under a lot of pressure."

"But why didn't you tell me?" I demanded. "Were you trying not to worry me?"

Mama hesitated. "You worry enough already."

I studied her. "But there's something else, isn't there?"

Mama shrugged. "I didn't think you were interested."

I put my arms around Mama. "I'm sorry, Mama, if I've been rotten. You don't have to do it all alone, you know."

Mama hugged me and then stepped back, her eyes flicking from my toes to the top of my head. "You're growing up."

By then, Stephanie came out of the kitchen empty-handed. "Do you know when my father will be here, Mrs. Chin?"

"He told me in about two hours," Mama said. She clapped her hands together. "I know. Let's have some of your special tea to celebrate."

"If you like," Stephanie winked at me.

"Let's get the special teapot?" Mama muttered. "Help me, Amy."

We went into the kitchen where I opened the cabinet.

Mama took it out, cradling it in her palms. "We aren't simple peasants. At one time, the Chins were quality."

"And still are," Stephanie said. She was having trouble not giggling. So was I. It was fun to share a secret with her.

"Open up the can of biscuits," she said.

Biscuits are what Mama called cookies. I got out the

tin can and arranged them on a plate. They were little cylinders and I set them out in concentric circles like rays.

Jason bopped in and immediately tried to use one as a telescope.

"They are not for playing," Mama said, filling a kettle with water.

"I'll get the tea," Stephanie said.

Mama went through her whole ritual, including heating the teapot gradually with hot water from the tap. Of course, I could now appreciate what a crucial step it was.

The kids and Mama had a good time at our tea. However, though Stephanie smiled, her heart didn't seem to be in it. I was feeling a little sad too.

We were just cleaning up when the doorbell rang. "I'll get it," Mama said, wiping her hands on a towel.

Stephanie took a deep breath and let it out slowly. "I guess the dream had to come to an end."

"We can have sleepovers," I promised.

"That would be nice," she said shyly.

"Welcome, Mr. Sinclair," Mama said from the hallway.

When I followed Stephanie to the hallway, I got my first look at Mr. Sinclair.

I guess I had expected him to be slender and fair like Stephanie. However, he was dumpy with legs and shoulders like someone who ought to be hauling crates on and off big ships.

"Hello, Stephie," Mr. Sinclair said, giving her a bone-crunching hug. "Have you been studying hard?"

I had expected him first to ask how she was. It seemed an odd question. No wonder Stephanie thought she had to be perfect.

"Yes, Father," Stephanie said.

As each of us was introduced, he gave a polite little nod and a smile instead of a hand shake. Perhaps he had picked that up in his Asian dealings.

"How was your trip, Father?" Stephanie asked with her usual good manners.

Mr. Sinclair laughed. "That Hong Kong bank tried to pull a few fast ones, but I was on to all their tricks." He pulled his lips back in a wolfish grin. "They won't try a hostile takeover again. What's mine is mine."

Up until then, he hadn't seemed all that remarkable. The grin made me think he showed another face to his business rivals.

"It always is," Stephanie said wearily—as if she had heard this many times before.

He lost the wolfish look for a puzzled one. "You make it sound like a problem."

Stephanie shrugged. "Well, you've certainly been very successful, Father." She glanced at me. "Is it all right if I stay? Amy and I had plans."

Mr. Sinclair was still friendly enough, but he was used to getting his own way. "I'm sure she'll understand if you have to leave. You do, don't you, Amy?"

"Of course she does," Mama said soothingly.

Stephanie bit her lip. "If you're going to be busy, I'll just be in the way at home."

Mr. Sinclair scratched his forehead. "You never seemed to mind before."

Stephanie stared down at her feet. "People change," she said softly. I think she was remembering what Madame had said about Cinderella.

"Of course they do," Mr. Sinclair said indulgently. "We'll talk about it at home."

Stephanie hesitated, glancing at me. I nodded encouragingly.

"No," Stephanie said quietly.

Mr. Sinclair rocked back on his heels. "What did you say?"

Stephanie's voice grew stronger. "No, Father."

Mr. Sinclair's eyebrows drew together in a thick, stormy line and I waited for a wolfish growl, but it only came out as a whine. "I thought you'd want to come home with me?"

Lifting her head, Stephanie dared to look back at her father. "I'd rather be here with the Chins than sitting by myself while you're on the telephone."

"But we'll do things." Mr. Sinclair said.

Stephanie folded her arms and challenged him. "Wonderful. What do you have planned for us? A show or a concert? A picnic?"

He shrugged sheepishly. "We'll think of something."

Stephanie tapped her fingers on her arms. "Who

else did you call from the airplane? Did you book the rest of the week for business appointments?"

Mr. Sinclair snapped his fingers. "We'll invite the Browns for dinner. You like them."

Stephanie shook her head. "They're your friends, not mine."

Mr. Sinclair stared in frustration at Stephanie as if he were realizing for the first time that his daughter had a mind of her own. "Then we'll have Lou-Lou over," Mr. Sinclair said.

"I detest Lou-Lou," Stephanie insisted.

Mr. Sinclair was surprised. "You do?"

"I told you where I'd rather be," Stephanie said. "Can't I stay for the original period like we planned?"

Mr. Sinclair glanced at Mama uncomfortably. "We don't want to impose on the Chins, Stephie. I think you should come home."

If he didn't have time for her, I couldn't see why he was so persistent.

"Am I a bother?" Stephanie asked Mama. A note of anxiety crept into her voice.

"None at all," Mama assured her.

Pivoting on her heel, Stephanie started to walk away.

Mr. Sinclair hurried after her. "Is that what you really want?"

Stephanie kept her back to him. "Yes."

"Well, if that's the way you want it . . ." he said uncertainly. He didn't look anything like a wolf now.

"I do," Stephanie said firmly.

"Have it your way, then," he snapped.

He started to turn when he looked through the doorway into the kitchen. "Where did you get that?"

"Get what?" Mama asked politely.

Mr. Sinclair strode into the kitchen and hovered over the drying rack. "That teapot."

"It's been in our family for generations," Mama declared proudly.

Mr. Sinclair looked thoughtful. "Oh, really? My wife had one just like that. It was very special to her."

"It's just gathering dust, Father," Stephanie said.

"I've been meaning to clean it," Mr. Sinclair said.

"Just have the maid do it," Stephanie said coolly.

"No, it's much too delicate," Mr. Sinclair insisted.

"I feel the same way about mine," Mama said.

Mr. Sinclair left right after that. I assumed he was in a hurry to conduct his business.

"Your father must have a lot on his mind," Mama said to Stephanie.

"It's not even because he needs the money anymore," Stephanie said. "He wants the challenge."

Mama tapped the side of her head. "I'd better put the teapot away before the children break it. I'd really hate that."

As she bustled into the kitchen, I leaned close to Stephanie and whispered. "Will your father notice that the teapot is missing?"

Stephanie made a face. "He won't. He'll be on the telephone as soon as he gets into our flat."

"But you just took it without asking him?" I asked.

Stephanie didn't seem very upset. "He said it was going to be mine some day. I just took it early."

"Maybe we'd better tell Mama the truth," I said.

Stephanie put her hand on my wrist. "And have her cut off your ballet lessons? Just leave everything to me."

"But your father seemed upset when he thought it was his teapot," I said. "He said it was special to your mother."

"Not that I ever knew. He only said that because he hates to lose anything that belongs to him," Stephanie said.

"Well, if he feels that way, what are you going to do?" I asked.

"I can always handle him," Stephanie said, as if her father were only three years old.

It was odd to feel sorry for Stephanie, but I did. I don't think I'd ever met anyone who was so alone.

EIGHTEEN

The Misunderstanding

A half hour later I answered the phone. It was Mr. Sinclair, but his voice could have froze the sun. "I want to speak to Stephanie right away."

I figure he was still mad about Stephanie preferring us to him. "I'll get her," I said.

I found her in the living room watching the Wolf Warriors with the kids. "Your father wants you."

"What now?" Stephanie sighed. She went into the hallway. "What is it, Father?" she asked impatiently. "What? I told you I'm staying. No. You can't do this. I won't go."

When she came back, she looked like she was ready to cry.

"Did your father change his mind about your staying?"

Stephanie nodded. Her voice was strained from the frustration. "He says he doesn't want me to spend another moment here."

"Why?" I asked.

"He said he'd tell me when he got here," Stephanie said.

"Do you think your father must checked for the teapot?" I whispered.

Stephanie chewed her lip. "He might have."

"We've got to tell him the truth," I said.

"And get you in trouble with your mother?" Stephanie asked in a low voice. "Do you want to give up ballet?"

"No, but I don't want my mother to go to jail, either," I said.

"She won't. I promise," Stephanie said.

I decided to take matters into my own hands. "Mama," I said, getting up.

"Don't," Stephanie said, trying to grab my hand to pull me back.

However, I went into the kitchen where Mama was washing some rice. "What is it?"

I swallowed, "It's about the teapot. I broke it. I'm sorry."

Mama smiled. "Don't joke about things like that. I handled it myself so I know it's not broken."

"Amy, don't," Stephanie said from the doorway, but I shook her off. Things had gone beyond covering up now.

"The teapot you have is Mr. Sinclair's. Stephanie and I replaced our broken one with his." I swallowed.

"I didn't say anything because I was afraid of upsetting you."

"And I was afraid of how you might punish Amy," Stephanie said. "It was really my fault. I was the one who put the boiling water into it."

I waited for Mama to rant and rave, but she simply stared at me. "You didn't warm the pot first?"

I swallowed. "No. I'm sorry."

Mama groaned. "The teapot was so fragile, you have to warm it before you put in boiling water."

"Remember when Stephanie first came and we used the teapot? I tried to ask why we had to put hot water in the pot. I wish you had told me," I said.

Mama gave a start. "I didn't, did I?"

My throat was suddenly dry. "What are we going to do, Mama?"

Mama massaged her forehead. "It's as much my fault as yours. I should have made you understand. But why didn't you tell me?"

"We were afraid you'd stop Amy's ballet lessons," Stephanie said.

She looked up at me suddenly. "Were you really that afraid of me?"

I shifted my feet uncomfortably.

Mama rocked back like I'd punched her in the stomach. "So you think I'm some monster."

She looked so sad that I gave her a hug. "No, Mama."

Mama squeezed me so hard she almost broke my ribs. "Really?"

Mama was a rock. She didn't seem to need anyone, so it was scary to see her this hungry for assurance. "Sure," I said.

We held onto one another for a long time. Then Mama patted me on the back. "You're more important than anything—even an old, dusty teapot."

I tilted back my head in surprise. "But it's the heirloom."

"No, you are." Mama nodded her head toward the living room where my brothers and sisters were watching television. "All of you are. The teapot was just a thing. A teapot can't hug back."

"I can't tell you how sorry I am," Stephanie said, finally stepping forward.

Mama let go of me with one last pat and then turned to Stephanie. "It's all right. We'll explain to your father that it's all a misunderstanding about the teapot."

Stephanie folded her arms as she stared down at her feet. "My father might be looking for a ring and a watch too."

"But you didn't give those to us," Mama said. She looked at me for confirmation. I shook my head.

Stephanie gave a little cough. "Not directly. When Papa goes away, he doesn't always remember to leave my allowance. So over the past few years, I've learned to take it in other forms besides money."

Mama asked in her gentlest, most non-threatening voice, "And how do you do that, Miss Stephanie?"

Stephanie clasped her hands behind her back. "I take things he's forgotten about and pawn them. In a way, it's like recycling," she said. "Up until now, he's never noticed. Usually he's too busy, and we move so often that if he does, my father figures it's in a box somewhere."

My jaw dropped open. So Cinderella really wasn't perfect after all. And neither was her fairy tale life.

"The comics, the meals—were those all 'other forms'?" Mama asked.

"He owed me the money," Stephanie said defensively.

"My clothes too?" I asked.

"No, those were already mine," Stephanie said. "I . . . I just didn't want them anymore."

"But—" I began to ask when Mama shot me a warning glance.

"All right then," Mama said calmly. "We'll give everything back to your father and pay for what we can't give back."

Stephanie jutted out her jaw stubbornly. "You really don't have to. The money really was due me. It's just that he can't be bothered about me. So I had to learn to take care of myself."

"That's not true, Miss Stephanie. Your father does care about you," Mama said.

Stephanie fidgeted with her sleeves. "When I was in the hospital, he hardly ever came."

"I'm sure he wanted to, but he was in too much pain," Mama said.

"When were you sick?" I asked.

"In Hong Kong," Stephanie said.

"Stephanie was in an . . . unfortunate accident," Mama said quickly.

Stephanie narrowed her eyebrows angrily. "That's not what Father thinks."

Mama swallowed. "You don't have to talk about it."

"No, it's Father who doesn't want to talk about it," Stephanie snapped. "He believes it's all my fault."

"He didn't say that!" Mama said, shocked.

"No," Stephanie bit off the word tensely. "I can see it in his face. I can see it in how he ignores me." She whirled around and said to me, "You were curious the other day about this." Stephanie dragged back her sleeve to show me the scar. "Do you really want to know how I got it?"

I felt like I was watching one of those horror movies. You know there's a monster waiting behind the door. You want to close your eyes or even leave the theater, but all you can do is sit and stare.

Stephanie held up a forearm so I could see the crescent scar better. "Well, I got this when I killed my mother."

I tried to talk but all my lips could stammer was, "W-what?"

"My father's had me see quacks ever since. He's afraid I'll do something crazy." she said, making a face. "Father doesn't dare send me to school. That's why I have tutors now."

"But your doctor says that you've been getting better," Mama was quick to say.

Stephanie laughed nervously. "Father still doesn't want to leave me alone."

"But he let you go to the ballet with me," I said.

Stephanie shrugged. "Your mother assured him you were responsible."

I didn't want to believe anything that Stephanie was telling me. I turned to Mama. "You knew all this when you took the job?"

Mama nodded.

I had misunderstood everything—from the reason why Mama had bent over backwards to please Stephanie to Stephanie's visit itself. And I had misunderstood Stephanie too—how eager she had been to please, how uncomfortable she had been with girls her own class and age.

"You don't have to be so alone. You could go to my school," I said.

"I'd still be in an invisible cage." Stephanie hugged herself. "Wherever I go. I can't help thinking when I meet someone, 'You don't know what a monster I am.'"

"You're no monster," I insisted. "My family loves you. You couldn't have killed anyone."

Stephanie was almost shaking. "But I did. It was in Hong Kong. Mother didn't want to take me to shopping, but I whined and whined until she gave in. If it hadn't been for me, that car wouldn't have hit us head on. We were both trapped inside the wreck. There was nothing I could do—except watch her die."

I pressed a hand beneath my throat. "That's awful." No wonder she'd needed to see doctors. I would have been a basket case.

"No one blames you," Mama said. "You're father just stays busy so that he doesn't have time to miss your mother. He doesn't mean to ignore you."

She held out an arm, inviting Stephanie in for a hug.

Stephanie, though, just stood there as if all she deserved was to be alone. So I went to her instead to give her a hug. "Remember what Madame said. There are two kinds of people—those who don't change and those who do. You've changed from that whiny girl."

Stephanie leaned her head against my shoulder. I was surprised when I felt something wet there. Stephanie was crying.

"I'd better pack my bag," she said, and fled down the hall.

NINETEEN

Freedom

Mama sent the kids to their room while we waited with Stephanie. Mr. Sinclair stormed into our flat an hour later. "You have some explaining to do," he said to Mama.

"It's all my fault," Stephanie interrupted. "I took everything." Next to her suitcase was the teapot wrapped in layers of newspaper.

Mr. Sinclair stood there embarrassed and hurt. "You what?"

"I broke the Chins' teapot so I replaced it with ours. And I took the other things because you didn't leave enough money for me," Stephanie said.

He frowned at her. "We'll discuss your behavior at home."

Stephanie nodded.

With a grunt, Mr. Sinclair turned to Mama. "I'm sorry about the misunderstanding."

Mama was standing in front of Stephanie who'd packed her bag. "It's all right. I'm just sorry that it happened."

Mr. Sinclair took out a check book. "Under the circumstances, I don't think we'll be needing your services anymore, Mrs. Chin. I'll write out a check for a month's severance pay."

"You can't do this, Father. It was all my fault," Stephanie protested and turned to me. "What about your lessons? How will you be able to afford them?"

Mama put a hand on my shoulder. "Don't worry," she told Stephanie. "We'll manage like we always have."

"I'm sorry," Mr. Sinclair said to Mama. "You understand."

"Of course," Mama said.

"Well, I don't," Stephanie said. "Why do we have to fire Mrs. Chin?"

"It's just the way things are," Mr. Sinclair said.

Whenever Mama said that, it made it sound like grown-ups belonged to a club with secret rules—ones that were frequently stupid. Ones that they never wanted to change.

It sounded to me like the Sinclairs were going to climb back into the canoe and paddle on down the river—until they went over the waterfall. I couldn't let that happen to Stephanie.

I thought again of what Madame had said. The Sinclairs were locked up in their own little world worse than the stepsisters. If anyone should know about all that, it should be me. I had played the stepsister in real life as well as in ballet. And if ever there was a time for change, this was one.

I pushed in front of Stephanie. "And what are you going to do?" I asked Mr. Sinclair. "Find another amah and go through the same thing all over again?"

"Amy!" Mama said, shocked.

Mr. Sinclair stared at me. "That's none of your business."

He might have been able to intimidate rich people around the world, but not me. "You wanted a Chinese amah. Well, you got one. And from what I understand, that means we're part of your family too." I jabbed a finger at myself. "That makes it my business."

Mama tried to pull me back. "That's enough, young lady."

I shook her off though. "No, Mama. We can't let them go on like this."

Mr. Sinclair jammed his hands into his pockets and leaned forward. "I believe that being her father puts me in a better position to know what's best for Stephanie."

I glared up at him. "Really? So who's her favorite movie star?"

"Uh . . ." Mr. Sinclair guessed. "Robert Redford?" He glanced at Stephanie for confirmation.

Stephanie shook her head with a slight smile.

I rolled my eyes. "Give her a break. He's old enough to be her grandfather."

Mr. Sinclair raised his shoulders in frustration.

"When do I have time to see a movie except on an airplane?"

"It's Jackie Chan, Father," Stephanie said.

"What's her favorite color? What's her favorite food?" I shot the questions at him. "If you really love your daughter, you'd know the answers." After all, Stephanie had done her homework on us.

"Kids' tastes change so fast nowadays," he said lamely.

"That's just my point," I said. "You don't have the time for Stephanie. We do."

"You don't understand the whole picture," he said.

"You used to have time," Stephanie said, and added softly, "when mother was alive."

Mr. Sinclair gave a little start at the mention of his wife—as if after all this time her memory still hurt him. "Things were different then. Business picked up after she died."

Mama gave him one of the same kind of radar looks she used on me when she caught me in a lie. "Or you decided to bury yourself in work."

Mr. Sinclair tilted back his head. "Really, Mrs. Chin. Keep your opinions to yourself."

Mama folded her arms and stood there like an immovable rock. "I would if I was an American governess because then I'd be nothing but an employee." Mama jerked her head at me. "Amy's right. You wanted a Chinese amah and that's what you got. Your family is my family now. I've seen enough to know what's going on. How long are you going to keep hiding in your business affairs?"

At that moment, I couldn't have been prouder of Mama, even if she couldn't fly like Mary Poppins.

Mr. Sinclair took his hands out of his pockets. "Everything I'm doing is for Stephanie."

Mama stepped in front of him so he had to look directly at her. "Why don't you ask Stephanie what she really wants?"

"Since you didn't want to come home with me, I assume the one thing you don't want is my company." He sounded as sulky as a small boy.

"I do when you're actually talking to me and not into a telephone," Stephanie said.

"Really?" He seemed pleasantly surprised. "Even if I like Robert Redford instead of Jackie Chan?"

"Even if," Stephanie smiled shyly.

He ran a hand through his hair. "Well, what would you like to do?"

"I'd like—" she began when something in Mr. Sinclair's pocket began to chirp.

Mr. Sinclair held up his hand apologetically. "Hold that thought." Taking out a cellular phone, he said into it, "Hello?"

As he listened to his caller, he became grim. "I don't take that from anyone," he said, starting to look wolfish.

Stephanie gave an exasperated sigh.

"Ahem," Mama said, clearing her throat noisily.

Mr. Sinclair glanced at her and became aware that we were all watching him. He pulled himself back from his wolf act. "Excuse me," he said suddenly into the telephone. "Call me tomorrow, will you?" He faced his daughter again. "Now what were you telling me?"

"I'd like Mrs. Chin to stay on," she said.

Mr. Sinclair put the phone into his pocket. "What do you think, Mrs. Chin?"

Mama hesitated. I don't think any of this was in the Official Amah's Handbook. "I don't know . . ."

Stephanie leaned her head to the side. "We might need a referee."

Mr. Sinclair pursed his lips thoughtfully and then nodded. "Please," he said to Mama. I don't think he was used to saying that word often. "This is going to be a long, slow process getting to know one another again. We'll need help."

I nudged Mama. "You know you want to stay on."

Mama surprised me, though, by turning to me. "What do you want, Amy?"

It was my turn to be surprised. "You really want to know?"

"I want a daughter who doesn't think her mama is a monster," she said.

It was like Mama had said before. Somehow we always managed and always would. We were those kind of people. Besides, I had learned to share Mama with my brothers and sisters. Two more wouldn't hurt.

"Stay on," I urged.

Mama wriggled her nose as if she had an itch. "We'll see how it goes."

Mr. Sinclair grinned at Stephanie. "We'd better behave. It sounds like we're on probation."

Stephanie smiled at her father. "Are you free today, Father?"

Mr. Sinclair hesitated for a moment as if he were turning over the pages of a planner inside his mind, but then he shook off those thoughts. "How am I going to pass another one of Amy's quizzes if I don't start learning about you?"

Stephanie started to take off her father's tie. "Then let's go somewhere together. What would you like to do?"

Mr. Sinclair leaned forward as his daughter drew it off. It was funny, but a man who knew how to bring off big business projects didn't have an idea. "I don't know. Leisure, what's that?"

"The park is nearby," I suggested. "It looks like a nice day for a walk."

As Mr. Sinclair straightened, he undid the top button of his shirt. "I'm so used to hotels that I don't know if I'm ready for fresh air."

Stephanie smiled at her father then she picked up

the teapot. She bowed to Mama and held it out to her. "I'm sorry about breaking your heirloom."

Mama wagged her hands from side to side. "I couldn't."

"I'm sorry that it doesn't have all the memories of the last one, but maybe it will bring you new ones," she said, and tried to hold it out again.

The two of them would have kept at it the rest of the day, wasting precious daylight time in the park. So I stepped in and took it. Ugly or not, it looked like I was going to be stuck with it one day. "Thanks. It's already brought us a memory of you, hasn't it?"

Mama scolded me. "Give that back."

"No backsies," Mr. Sinclair laughed.

Stephanie turned and hugged Mama. "I know this won't all be easy, but thank you."

"Just remember," Mama said, "you have us."

"Not that we're perfect either," I laughed.

Stephanie let go of Mama and wrapped her arms around me. "That's the whole point, isn't it? If you were perfect to begin with, why would you want to improve?"

"We can keep trying to get better together," I agreed.

Mr. Sinclair took Stephanie by the arm. "Now if you'll excuse us, we have an important appointment with some pigeons."

Mama and I both went to the living room window

and looked through the blinds. Stephanie and her father were walking arm and arm to the park.

I gave a sigh. Still cradling the teapot, I crossed my fingers for them. "It's a new start. I hope it works."

"So do I," Mama sighed, letting go of the blind slats.

I set the teapot carefully down on a table. "Mama, do you love Stephanie?"

"You said it yourself. She's part of our family," Mama replied.

I hesitated but I couldn't help asking, "More than me?"

Mama stared at me. "You get the strangest notions. Whatever made you think that?"

I shrugged. "Lots of things."

"Such as," Mama demanded.

"I don't know." A lot of what Mama had said and done could be explained now that I knew Stephanie's condition.

Mama clasped her hands behind her back. "I would really like to know."

I drew a finger along the side of the teapot. "You just seemed to understand her better than the rest of us."

I cringed, waiting for the scolding, but Mama didn't say anything.

So I risked a glance at her. She was looking thoughtful.

"Maybe it's because I was trying harder," Mama admitted.

"It was your job," I said charitably.

She took my hand. "But I could try harder with you. This is such a strange country to me, and there's so much I don't understand. So sometimes I make mistakes with you children."

I thought of how strong Mama had been—how she had tried to protect us and Stephanie in different ways. She might not do everything the way an American mother would, but that didn't mean she didn't love us.

"Maybe Mr. Sinclair isn't the only one who has to learn about his family." Mama gave my hand a squeeze. "I won't make promises either, but let's try."

"Where's Stephanie?" Mimi asked from the doorway.

"She had to leave," Mama explained.

"Oh," Mimi said in a small, disappointed voice.

It's funny when you see people through someone else's eyes. Jason, Mimi, Didi and Andy weren't pests at all to Stephanie. So maybe I'd never be a Stephanie to them, but I could at least try not to be a mean old stepsister.

I put my hands on my knees as I leaned forward and looked at her. "So who's up for ice cream?"

"Me," Andy shouted from the hallway and thundered toward us. Didi and Jason echoed him.

Mama joined in. "Me." She picked up her wallet. "And while we're out, we'll get a pattern for your costume."

So she hadn't forgotten after all. Suddenly there were all these warm little bubbles inside. I felt as if I were no longer trapped . . . as if a door had suddenly opened in the cage. I felt free.

"Then let's go," I said.

There was a whole world waiting outside for us. I started looking for my coat.